GRAPHIC SHAKESPEARE

SALARIYA
BH
BOOK HOUSE

Contents

Hamlet
Prince of Denmark

William Shakespeare

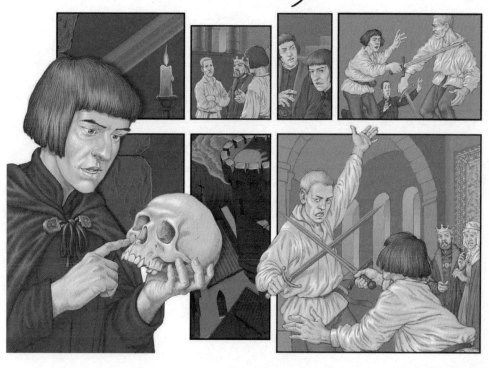

Illustrated by

Penko Gelev

Retold by

Kathy McEvoy

Series created and designed by

David Salariya

The castle of Elsinore in Denmark, some time in the twelfth century.

The old king, Hamlet, has recently died. He has been succeeded not by his son, Prince Hamlet, but by his brother Claudius.

Claudius has married Gertrude, who is the old king's widow and Prince Hamlet's mother.

CHARACTERS

Hamlet,
Prince of Denmark

The Ghost of old Hamlet,
late King of Denmark,
Prince Hamlet's father

Claudius, new King of Denmark,
Hamlet's uncle and stepfather

Gertrude, Queen of Denmark,
Hamlet's mother

Horatio,
Hamlet's friend from university

Polonius,
a courtier

Ophelia,
Polonius' daughter

Laertes,
Polonius' son

Fortinbras,
Prince of Norway

Rosencrantz and Guildenstern,
friends of Hamlet from childhood

A gravedigger

A WEIRD VISITOR

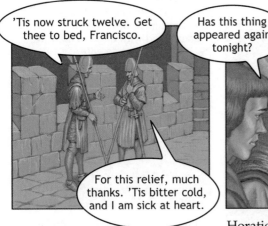

'Tis now struck twelve. Get thee to bed, Francisco.

For this relief, much thanks. 'Tis bitter cold, and I am sick at heart.

At midnight, the soldiers change guard on the battlements.

Has this thing appeared again tonight?

I have seen nothing.

Horatio has come to investigate two reported sightings of a ghost in recent nights.

Horatio says 'tis but our fantasy, and will not let belief take hold of him. Therefore I have entreated him along.[1]

Horatio does not believe in ghosts.

Peace, break thee off. Look, where it comes again!

In the same figure,[2] like the king that's dead.

They begin to tell Horatio about the ghost when suddenly…

What art thou that usurp'st[3] this time of night? By heaven I charge thee, speak!

Horatio challenges the ghost, but it turns and disappears.

Is it not like the king?

As thou art to thyself.[4]

They all agree that the ghost looks very much like old Hamlet, who has just died.

…to recover of us… those foresaid lands so by his father lost.

Is it a warning that Prince Fortinbras of Norway plans to invade Denmark?

Stay, illusion! If thou hast any sound, or use of voice, speak to me.

The ghost reappears, and again Horatio tries to speak to it, but a cock crows. The ghost vanishes. It's dawn.

Let us impart what we have seen tonight unto young Hamlet. For, upon my life, this spirit, dumb to us, will speak to him.

1. entreated him along: convinced him to come along.   2. In the same figure: In the same shape and form (as the old king).
3. usurp'st: invades or wrongfully takes over.   4. As thou art to thyself: As real as you are to yourself.

An Unhappy Prince

Though yet of Hamlet our dear brother's death the memory be green[1]...

Claudius is addressing the court and visitors who have come for the old king's funeral. Many still mourn him.

Our sometime sister,[2] now our queen, have we, with mirth in funeral and with dirge in marriage,[3] taken to wife.

Claudius explains that, although he is grief-stricken, his marriage to Gertrude will keep the kingdom stable.

Nor have we herein barr'd your better wisdoms,[4] which have freely gone with this affair along.

He thanks everyone for their good wishes and support.

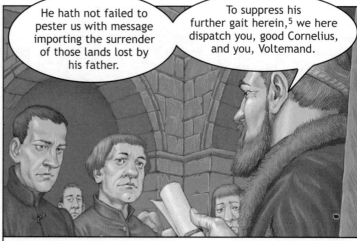

He hath not failed to pester us with message importing the surrender of those lands lost by his father.

To suppress his further gait herein,[5] we here dispatch you, good Cornelius, and you, Voltemand.

He sends two ambassadors to Norway to negotiate with young Fortinbras, who threatens to invade.

You told us of some suit. What is't, Laertes?

My dread lord, your leave and favour[6] to return to France.

Laertes, the son of Polonius, wishes to return to his studies in France.

Have you your father's leave? What says Polonius?

He hath, my lord, wrung from me my slow leave by laboursome petition.[7]

Claudius asks Polonius if he is in favour...

Take thy fair hour, Laertes. Time be thine, and thy best graces spend it at thy will.

...and agrees to let Laertes go.

---

1. green: fresh.   2. sometime sister: former sister-in-law.   3. with . . . marriage: with joy and sorrow at the same time.
4. barr'd your better wisdoms: ignored your good advice.   5. to suppress his further gait herein: to stop his progress.
6. leave and favour: permission.   7. laboursome petition: persistent requests.

But now, my cousin Hamlet, and my son — How is it that the clouds still hang on you?

Claudius questions Hamlet about his deep depression since his father's death.

A little more than kin, and less than kind.

'Cousin? Son?' mutters Hamlet: we may be related now, but we are not alike.

Good Hamlet, cast thy nighted colour off.[1] All that lives must die, passing through nature to eternity.

Gertrude tells her son that the time for grieving and wearing black is over, and he should welcome Claudius.

But I have that within which passes show — these but the trappings and the suits of woe.[2]

Hamlet's grief is locked inside him, whatever colour he wears.

To persever[3] in obstinate condolement[4] is a course of impious stubbornness.

Hamlet is accused of over-reacting – he should accept that death is a natural end.

Throw to earth this unprevailing woe.[5]

Let not thy mother lose her prayers[6] — stay with us. Go not to Wittenberg.

Claudius and Gertrude beg Hamlet not to return to university in Wittenberg.

I shall in all my best obey you, madam.

Reluctantly, Hamlet agrees.

1. cast . . . off: remove your mourning clothes.   2. suits of woe: mourning clothes.   3. persever: persevere, persist.
4. obstinate condolement: stubborn, continuous mourning.   5. Throw . . . woe: End this grief, no good will come of it.
6. lose her prayers: beg in vain.

A FRIEND IN NEED

O, that this too too solid flesh would melt, thaw and resolve itself into a dew. Or that the Everlasting had not fixed his canon 'gainst self-slaughter![1]

Hamlet is so unhappy he wants to die and disappear. Suicide would solve his problems – but it is a sin.

Frailty, thy name is woman!

How could his mother marry barely a month after his father's death?

Within a month... My father's brother, but no more like my father than I to Hercules.

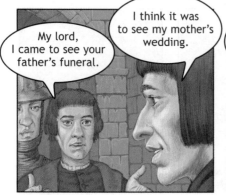

My lord, I came to see your father's funeral.

I think it was to see my mother's wedding.

But just then Horatio and the soldiers burst in. Hamlet is glad to see his friend. He's sarcastic about the hasty marriage.

Indeed, my lord, it followed hard upon.

The funeral baked meats did coldly furnish forth the marriage tables.[2]

My lord, I think I saw him yesternight.[3]

Saw? Who?

My lord, the king your father.

And then Horatio tells Hamlet about the ghost he has seen.

Thrice he walked by their oppressed and fear-surprised eyes!

I will watch tonight, perchance 'twill walk again.

Hamlet will keep watch himself tonight. Perhaps the ghost wants to warn him of something.

My father's spirit in arms![4] All is not well... Foul deeds will rise, though all the earth o'erwhelm them to men's eyes.[5]

Hamlet suspects the ghost's appearance has something to do with his father's death.

1. fixed . . . self-slaughter: forbidden suicide.   2. The funeral . . . tables: The leftover food from the funeral was served cold at the wedding.   3. yesternight: last night.   4. in arms: wearing armour.   5. Foul . . . eyes: Evil deeds will be found out, however carefully they are hidden.

Laertes prepares to leave for France. He is very close to his sister Ophelia and is sorry to leave her.

He warns her that Hamlet's feelings for her cannot be trusted.

Polonius now gives his son some fatherly advice: always be honest to yourself...

...and others. Laertes sets off for France.

Polonius has overheard Laertes mention Hamlet. He questions Ophelia about the prince.

Angered, he forbids her to meet or talk with Hamlet. Meekly she obeys.

---

1. My necessaries are embarked: My belongings have been loaded on board ship.   2. the trifling of his favour: the unreliability of his affections.   3. a toy in blood: a whim of passion.   4. weigh what loss your honour may sustain: consider how much honour you may lose.   5. with too credent ear: too trustingly.   6. list: listen to   7. tenders: offers, expressions.   8. green: inexperienced, naïve.   9. slander any moment leisure: waste any of your time.

THE GHOST WALKS AGAIN

The clock strikes midnight.

It then draws near the season[1] wherein the spirit held his wont to walk.

Hamlet and his friends await the ghost on the battlements.

The sound of gunshots and a loud party is coming from the castle below.

The king doth wake tonight and takes his rouse.[2]

They clepe[3] us drunkards.

Hamlet is disgusted. His uncle's drunken and rowdy behaviour is giving Denmark a bad reputation.

Look, my lord, it comes!

Suddenly, the ghost appears!

I'll call thee Hamlet, King, father, royal Dane.

O answer me!

Hamlet speaks to his father's ghost.

It beckons you to go away with it, as if it some impartment did desire[4] to you alone.

Do not go with it.

What if it tempt you toward the flood, my lord, or to the dreadful summit of the cliff?

Unhand me, gentlemen! By heaven, I'll make a ghost of him that lets[5] me!

The others try to restrain him but Hamlet follows the ghost.

Something is rotten in the state of Denmark. Let's follow him.

1. draws near the season: comes close to the time.   2. takes his rouse: is celebrating.
12   3. clepe: call.   4. some impartment did desire: wanted to say something.   5. lets: hinders.

I am thy father's spirit, doomed for a certain term to walk the night.

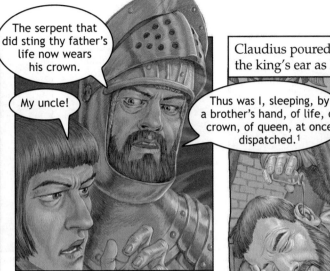

The serpent that did sting thy father's life now wears his crown.

My uncle!

The king was killed by a 'snake': his own brother!

Claudius poured poison into the king's ear as he slept.

Thus was I, sleeping, by a brother's hand, of life, of crown, of queen, at once dispatched.[1]

Taint not thy mind, nor let thy soul contrive against thy mother aught. Leave her to heaven.

Adieu, adieu, adieu. Remember me.

Never make known what you have seen tonight.

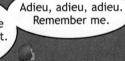

Thy commandment all alone shall live within the book and volume of my brain.[2]

At dawn the ghost vanishes. Hamlet's suspicions are correct.

The time is out of joint.[4] O cursed spite, that ever I was born to set it right!

There are more things in heaven and earth, Horatio, than are dreamt of in your philosophy.

I perchance hereafter shall think meet to put an antic disposition on.[3]

Horatio can hardly believe what they've seen. Hamlet warns them that his behaviour may become erratic.

With threats of an imminent invasion from Norway, can Hamlet avenge his father's murder?

1. dispatched: deprived.   2. within . . . brain: shall fill my mind.   3. think meet to put an antic disposition on: feel the need to act strangely.   4. The time is out of joint: The situation is bad.

Is Hamlet Mad?

Polonius is sending a servant to France to visit Laertes.

He wants to check up on Laertes.

Ophelia has just seen Hamlet. His strange behaviour has frightened her.

Ophelia has been avoiding Hamlet, as her father ordered.

Has he misjudged Hamlet after all?

The king must be told about this at once!

1. with his doublet all unbraced: with his jacket undone.　2. He falls . . . draw it: He studies my face as if he were trying to draw it.　3. repel: refuse to take.　4. beshrew my jealousy: shame on my suspiciousness.

Welcome, dear Rosencrantz and Guildenstern!

The need we have to use you did provoke our hasty sending.[1]

I entreat you both...

...to gather, so much as from occasion you may glean, whether aught to us unknown afflicts him thus.

Sure I am two men there is not living to whom he more adheres.[2]

Claudius wants Hamlet's old friends to find out what's wrong with him.

Is Hamlet upset about something unknown to Claudius?

They are, after all, Hamlet's closest friends.

Your visitation shall receive such thanks as befits a king's remembrance...

And their efforts will be rewarded...

Thanks, Guildenstern and gentle Rosencrantz.

The ambassadors from Norway are joyfully returned...

...and I have found the very cause of Hamlet's lunacy.

As they leave, Polonius arrives with news.

Say, Voltemand, what from our brother Norway?[3]

Most fair return of greetings and desires.

...never more to give the assay of arms[4] against your majesty.

...that it might please you to give quiet pass through your dominions.

The ambassadors have been successful. The king of Norway has made Prince Fortinbras promise not to attack Denmark.

Fortinbras asks for safe passage through Denmark on his way to fight the Poles.

1. did . . . sending: made us send for you quickly.   2. to whom he more adheres: whom he trusts more.
3. our brother Norway: the king of Norway.   4. to give the assay of arms: to use weapons.

15

MAD OR LOVESICK?

He tells me... he hath found the head and source of all your son's distemper.[1]

Polonius thinks he can explain Hamlet's behaviour.

'Doubt thou the stars are fire, doubt that the sun doth move...

He reads them a letter received by Ophelia.

'Doubt truth to be a liar, but never doubt I love.'

Came this from Hamlet to her?

'Lord Hamlet is a prince out of thy star.[2] This must not be.'

He had told Ophelia to give Hamlet up because she could never marry a Prince.

And he, repelled[3]... fell into a sadness, then... into the madness wherein now he raves.

He thinks Ophelia's rejection has driven Hamlet mad.

You know, sometimes he walks four hours together here in the lobby.

He suggests that they set a trap for Hamlet, to spy on him.

At such a time I'll loose my daughter to him. Be you and I behind an arras[4] then.

But look, where sadly the poor wretch comes reading.

Away, I do beseech you[5] both, away.

1. distemper: strange behaviour.   2. out of thy star: not in your destiny.   3. repelled: rejected by Ophelia.
4. arras: tapestry wall hanging (made at Arras in northern France).   5. beseech you: beg you

"Do you know me, my lord?"

"Excellent well. You are a fishmonger."

Polonius soon sees for himself Hamlet's strange behaviour.

"What do you read, my lord?"

"Words, words, words."

"Yourself, sir, shall grow old as I am, if like a crab you could go backward."

"Though this be madness, yet there is method in't."

Polonius suspects there's something behind this nonsense.

"My honourable lord, I will most humbly take my leave of you."

"You cannot, sir, take from me anything that I will more willingly part withal,[1] except my life."

Rosencrantz and Guildenstern have managed to find Hamlet.

"How dost thou, Guildenstern? Ah, Rosencrantz! Good lads, how do ye both?"

Their sudden visit makes Hamlet suspicious.

"What make you[2] at Elsinore?"

"To visit you, my lord, no other occasion."

"There is a kind of confession in your looks which your modesties[3] have not craft enough to colour.[4]"

"He that plays the king shall be welcome..."

To distract him, they announce the arrival of his favourite troupe of strolling actors.

"You are welcome, but my uncle-father and aunt-mother are deceived."

"I am mad but north-north-west. When the wind is southerly I know a hawk from a handsaw.[5]"

Hamlet informs them that he knows what they're up to.

1. withal: with.   2. What make you?: What are you doing?
3. modesties: sense of shame.   4. have not craft enough to colour: are not crafty enough to hide.   5. I know a hawk from a handsaw: I know what's what.

THE ACTORS

Polonius announces the actors. They can perform any style of acting you can name.

The best actors in the world, either for tragedy, comedy, history, pastoral...

Pray God, your voice, like a piece of uncurrent[1] gold, be not cracked within the ring.[2]

Hamlet teases the boy who plays the women's parts – soon his voice will break.

Come, give us a taste of your quality. Come, a passionate speech.

Hamlet is impatient for them to begin.

Look where he has not turned his colour and has tears in's eyes.

The lead actor performs a stirring speech from *The Trojan War*, with tears in his eyes.

Polonius is ordered to take good care of the actors.

Let them be well used, for they are the abstract and brief chronicles of the time.[3]

My lord, I will use them according to their desert.[4]

Like most people, Polonius looks down on actors. Hamlet reminds him that they deserve respect.

Dost thou hear me, old friend? Can you play *The Murder of Gonzago*?

Ay, my lord.

You could for a need study a speech of some dozen or sixteen lines, which I would set down and insert in't, could you not?

Ay, my lord.

Hamlet speaks to the lead actor and sets his plan in motion. He has chosen tomorrow night's play very carefully...

1. uncurrent: without value.   2. cracked within the ring: broken (a reference to the fact that a coin of the time would be made worthless if it was cracked from the edge to the ring surrounding the monarch's portrait).   3. abstract . . . time: short summary of the way things are.   4. use them according to their desert: treat them as they deserve.

Is it not monstrous that this player here, but in a fiction, in a dream of passion...

...could force his soul so to his own conceit that from her working all his visage wanned.[1]

Left alone, Hamlet bursts out angrily.

How can an actor feign such real passion?

What would he do, had he the motive and the cue for passion that I have? He would drown the stage with tears.

He compares his own situation.

Yet I, a dull and muddy-mettled[2] rascal, peak,[3] like John-a-dreams,[4] unpregnant of my cause,[5] and can say nothing.

Why can't he take action?

Am I a coward? That I, the son of a dear father murdered... must, like a whore, unpack my heart with words[6]...

I have heard that guilty creatures sitting at a play have, by the very cunning of the scene...

...been struck so to the soul that presently they have proclaimed their malefactions.[7]

I'll have these players play something like the murder of my father before mine uncle... If he do blench,[8] I know my course.

If Claudius' reaction to the play betrays guilt, Hamlet will know what to do.

This is the answer!

The play's the thing wherein I'll catch the conscience of the king.

1. all his visage wanned: his whole face grew pale.   2. muddy-mettled: dull-spirited.   3. peak: mope.
4. John-a-dreams: nickname for a dreamy person.   5. unpregnant of my cause: slow to act.   6. unpack my heart with words: do nothing but talk.   7. malefactions: wrong-doings.   8. blench: flinch and turn aside.

A Trap is Set

He does confess he feels himself distracted, but from what cause he will by no means speak.

Rosencrantz and Guildenstern admit that they do not know what is wrong with Hamlet.

Nor do we find him forward to be sounded[1] but, with a crafty madness, keeps aloof.

It so fell out that certain players we o'er-raught[2] on the way. And there did seem in him a kind of joy.

They tell the queen that the actor's passion pleased Hamlet.

They have already order this night to play before him.

Claudius is glad to hear about the play.

Sweet Gertrude, leave us too, for we have closely[3] sent for Hamlet hither, that he, as 'twere by accident, may here affront[4] Ophelia.

But now it's time to put Polonius' plan into action.

Her father and myself, lawful espials,[5] will so bestow[6] ourselves that, seeing unseen, we may of their encounter frankly judge.

I hear him coming. Let's withdraw, my lord.

They'll see if Hamlet has gone mad out of love for Ophelia.

Read on this book, that show of such an exercise may colour your loneliness.[7]

We are oft to blame in this, that with devotion's visage[8] and pious action we do sugar o'er the devil himself.[9]

Polonius is reminded that people often conceal badness by pretending to be good.

O, 'tis too true! How smart a lash that speech doth give my conscience!

These words strike a chord with Claudius!

1. forward to be sounded: eager to be questioned.   2. o'er-raught: overtook.   3. closely: privately, secretly.
4. affront: come face to face with.   5. espials: spies.   6. bestow: position.   7. show . . . loneliness: if you pretend to read, Hamlet will not think it odd that you are by yourself.   8. devotion's visage: an appearance of devoutness.
9. sugar . . . himself: hide bad deeds with sweetness.

Hamlet's distress and confusion continues. Is it worth living?

Is dying any worse than going to sleep?

But what may happen after death – nightmares?

The problems of life could be ended so quickly.

The fear of what happens after death makes people live with their problems, rather than taking their own life.

The turmoil in his mind prevents him from taking his revenge.

1. to be or not to be: to live or to die.   2. there's the rub: that's the problem.   3. his quietus make: free himself.
4. a bare bodkin: a mere dagger.   5. puzzles the will: stops us in confusion.

Not Mad For Love

The fair Ophelia! Nymph, in thy orisons[1] be all my sins remembered.

Just then, he sees Ophelia. He thinks she is reading a prayerbook.

My lord, I have remembrances[2] of yours that I have longed long to re-deliver.

She tries to return his letters and love tokens.

She recalls happier times.

Take these again, for to the noble mind rich gifts wax poor[3] when givers prove unkind.

I did love you once.

Indeed, my lord, you made me believe so.

But then he turns on her.

Get thee to a nunnery. Why wouldst thou be a breeder of sinners?

We are arrant knaves[4] all, believe none of us.

O, help him, you sweet heavens!

Or if thou wilt needs marry, marry a fool...

...for wise men know well enough what monsters you make of them.

Hamlet blames all women for men's unhappiness. They should become nuns and have no more children. He's really thinking about his mother.

God hath given you one face and you make yourselves another.

Women use make-up to trick men.

I say we will have no more marriage. Those that are married already, all but one shall live[5] — the rest shall keep as they are.

His feelings all relate to his mother.

1. orisons: prayers.   2. remembrances: keepsakes, gifts.   3. wax poor: become worthless.
4. arrant knaves: despicable men.   5. all but one shall live: all married couples but one shall live on. Hamlet is referring to Claudius and Gertrude. He intends to end their marriage violently.

To a nunnery, go.

O, what a noble mind is here o'erthrown! O, woe is me, t'have seen what I have seen.

Love! His affections do not that way tend, nor what he spake, though it lacked form a little,[1] was not like madness.

Claudius now knows that Hamlet is not in love with Ophelia – but neither is he mad.

There's something in his soul, o'er which his melancholy sits on brood.[2]

Claudius knows that trouble lies ahead.

I have in quick determination thus set it down: he shall with speed to England.

He decides to get rid of Hamlet by sending him to England.

After the play, let his queen mother all alone entreat[3] him to show his grief...

...and I'll be placed, so please you, in the ear of all their conference.[4]

It shall be so. Madness in great ones must not unwatch'd go.

Polonius is still not convinced. He has another plan. Perhaps the queen can persuade Hamlet to reveal his problem?

Reluctantly, Claudius agrees.

---

1. lacked form a little: made little sense.   2. sits on brood: broods over, like a hen hatching eggs.
3. entreat: beg.   4. in the ear of all their conference: within earshot of their conversation.

THE PLAY

Hamlet wants the actors to behave naturally and not to overact or shout.

Horatio must watch Claudius carefully during the murder scene.

In the play, the queen declares she would never marry again, but the king says he knows better.

Claudius is getting uneasy.

Claudius stops the play.

1. trippingly on the tongue: as you would speak naturally.   2. prithee: beg you.   3. argument: the plot of the play.
4. Is there no offence in't?: Are you sure there's nothing insulting in it?   5. anon: soon.

This convinces Hamlet that the ghost told the truth.

O good Horatio, didst perceive?[1]...

...upon the talk of the poisoning?

Very well, my lord.

Come, some music! Come, the recorders!

The king, sir, is in his retirement marvellous distempered.[2]

The king and queen are upset.

The queen...in most great affliction of spirit,[3] hath sent me to you.

She desires to speak with you in her closet[4] ere[5] you go to bed.

Good my lord, what is your cause of distemper?

Sir, I lack advancement.[6]

Asked to explain himself, Hamlet pretends he's angry at not inheriting the throne.

O, the recorders.

Will you play upon this pipe?

My lord, I cannot.

He teases Rosencrantz and Guildenstern.

'Tis as easy as lying — give it breath with your mouth and it will discourse most eloquent music.

Why, look you now, how unworthy a thing you make of me!

You would play upon me — do you think I am easier to be played on than a pipe?

Hamlet reveals that he knows what they have been up to.

I will speak daggers[7] to her, but use none.

Hamlet must speak plainly to his mother, but vows not to harm her, despite his anger.

1. didst perceive?: did you see?   2. distempered: angry.   3. affliction of spirit: dismay.
4. closet: private room.   5. ere: before.   6. I lack advancement: I am not moving up in the world (i.e. I am not king).
7. speak daggers: speak angrily.

Mistaken Identity

Claudius tells Rosencrantz and Guildenstern that they must take Hamlet to England. He's a danger to the kingdom.

Polonius plans to spy on Hamlet and his mother.

Claudius reflects on his guilt. A brother's murder is a terrible sin!

Seeing Claudius at prayer, Hamlet contemplates murder.

But he decides against killing Claudius in prayer.

Claudius knows that his prayers are in vain.

Speech (panel 1): I like him not, nor stands it safe with us to let his madness range.

He to England shall along with you.

Speech (panel 2): My lord, he's going to his mother's closet. Behind the arras I'll convey myself, to hear the process.[1]

Speech (panel 3): O, my offence is rank; it smells to heaven. It hath the primal eldest curse[2] upon't, a brother's murder.

Speech (panel 4): But, O, what form of prayer can serve my turn?

'Forgive me my foul murder'?

Speech (panel 5): O wretched state! O bosom black as death! O limed[3] soul that, struggling to be free, art more engaged!

Speech (panel 6): And now I'll do't. And so he goes to heaven. And so am I revenged.

Speech (panel 7): And am I then revenged, to take him in the purging of his soul, when he is fit and seasoned for his passage?[4]

No!

...that his soul may be as damned and black as hell, whereto it goes.

Speech (panel 8): My words fly up, my thoughts remain below.

Words without thoughts never to heaven go.

1. process: what goes on.
2. primal eldest curse: refers to Cain's murder of his brother Abel in the Bible.
3. limed: stuck in a trap.
4. to take . . . passage: to kill him in prayer, when his soul is cleansed and fit to go to heaven.

Tell him... your grace hath screen'd and stood between much heat and him.[1] I'll silence me e'en here.

Hamlet, thou hast thy father[2] much offended.

Mother, you have my father[3] much offended.

Hamlet refuses to refer to his stepfather Claudius as 'father'.

Gertrude is afraid of Hamlet.

You go not till I set you up a glass[4] where you may see the inmost part of you.

Thou wilt not murder me?

What, ho! Help, help!

How now! A rat?

O, I am slain!

The queen is horrified.

O, what a rash and bloody deed is this!

A bloody deed! Almost as bad, good mother, as kill a king and marry with his brother.

Hamlet has killed Polonius.

Intruding fool, farewell! I took thee for thy better.

Look here, upon this picture, and on this. This was your husband. Look you now, what follows.

He points to portraits of his father and uncle. How could she love Claudius?

Do not forget:

This visitation is but to whet thy almost blunted purpose.[5]

Do you see nothing there?

The ghost reminds Hamlet of his promise. Now Gertrude fears Hamlet really is mad.

O Hamlet, thou hast cleft my heart in twain.[6]

O, throw away the worser part of it, and live the purer with the other half.

1. your grace . . . him: you have protected him from a lot of trouble.
2. thy father: she means Claudius.   3. my father: he means old Hamlet.   4. set you up a glass: get you a mirror.
5. to whet thy almost blunted purpose: to remind Hamlet to aim his revenge at Claudius.
6. cleft my heart in twain: cut my heart in two.

27

HAMLET MUST GO

When Claudius hears of Polonius' death, he realises that Hamlet cannot be left on the loose much longer.

> O heavy deed! It had been so with us,[1] had we been there.

> This vile deed we must with all our majesty and skill both countenance[2] and excuse.

> Hamlet in madness hath Polonius slain, and from his mother's closet hath he dragged him.

> Go seek him out.

Claudius is concerned that he will be blamed for this tragedy.

> This sudden sending him away must seem deliberate pause[3]...

> Diseases desperate grown by desperate appliance are relieved, or not at all.

Claudius has to get rid of Hamlet, but it must look convincing.

> Where is Polonius?

> In heaven — send thither to see.

Hamlet taunts Claudius by answering him flippantly, in riddles.

> If your messenger find him not there, seek him i'th'other place[4] yourself.

> But indeed, if you find him not...you shall nose[5] him as you go up the stairs into the lobby.

> Hamlet, this deed, for thine especial safety...must send thee hence with fiery quickness.

Claudius claims he is sending Hamlet away for his own safety.

> The bark[6] is ready and the wind at help. The associates tend, and everything is bent for England.

> For England?

A ship is waiting to take him to England right away.

> Our sovereign process,[7] which imports at full[8]...

> ...the present death of Hamlet.

A secret letter instructs the king of England to have Hamlet murdered!

1. It had been so with us: He would have killed me.   2. countenance: accept.
3. pause: consideration.   4. th'other place: hell.   5. nose: smell.   6. bark: ship.
7. sovereign process: royal order.   8. imports at full: gives full instructions for.

Go, captain, from me greet the Danish king.

Fortinbras craves the conveyance of a promised march over his kingdom.

The Norwegian army is marching across Denmark, as arranged earlier.

Good sir, whose powers are these? How purposed?[1]

They are of Norway, sir, against some part of Poland.

Truly to speak...we go to gain a little patch of ground...

How all occasions do inform against me, and spur my dull revenge!

...that hath in it no profit but the name.

On the way to the harbour, Hamlet meets some soldiers.

The captain admits that their mission is fairly pointless.

To my shame, I see the imminent death of twenty thousand men...

I do not know why yet I live to say 'This thing's to do.'[2]

...sith[3] I have cause and will and strength and means to do't.

...that, for a fantasy and trick of fame, go to their graves like beds.

O, from this time forth...

...my thoughts be bloody, or be nothing worth!

Why can't he just get on with it?

He vows to act.

1. whose . . . purposed?: whose army is this? What is their mission?
2. This thing's to do: This thing has yet to be done.   3. sith: since.

29

OPHELIA'S TRAGEDY

Back at court, Ophelia begs to see the queen.

I will not speak with her.

She is importunate, indeed distract.[1]

The shock of her father's death has affected her mind.

'He is dead and gone, lady, He is dead and gone. At his head a grass-green turf, At his heels a stone.'

'Tomorrow is Saint Valentine's day, All in the morning betime,[2] And I a maid at your window, To be your Valentine.'

Pretty Ophelia!

Even Claudius is affected by Ophelia's distress.

Follow her close. Give her good watch,[3] I pray you.

O, this is the poison of deep grief. It springs all from her father's death.

When sorrows come, they come not single spies but in battalions.[4] First, her father slain...

Next, your son gone...poor Ophelia.

The situation worsens. One tragedy follows another.

Laertes has returned...

Last, and as much containing as all these,[5] her brother is in secret come from France...

...and it seems he blames Claudius for his father's death.

...and wants not buzzers[6] to infect his ear with pestilent speeches[7] of his father's death.

There's a commotion outside.

Save yourself, my lord. Young Laertes, in a riotous head, o'erbears your officers.

They cry, 'Choose we:[8] Laertes shall be king!'

---

1. importunate, indeed distract: insisting, in fact out of her mind.   2. betime: early.
3. Give her good watch: Watch her carefully.   4. they come . . . battalions: (sorrows) come one after the other.
5. Last, and . . . these: Last, but not least.   6. wants not buzzers: is not short of rumour-mongers.
7. pestilent speeches: disrespectful talk.   8. Choose we: Let us choose.

O thou vile king, give me my father!

Before they can move, Laertes bursts in.

Tell me, Laertes, why thou art thus incensed.

Claudius calms him down.

Where is my father?

Dead.

But not by him.

Is't possible a young maid's wits should be as mortal as[1] an old man's life?

Before he can explain, Ophelia appears once again.

There's rosemary, that's for remembrance...

...and there is pansies, that's for thoughts.

I would give you some violets, but they withered all when my father died.

Laertes can't believe what he is seeing.

Do you see this, O God?

If by direct or by collateral hand they find us touched,[2] we will our kingdom give.

Claudius says others should judge whether he was involved in Polonius' death.

His means of death, his obscure funeral[3]...cry to be heard. I must call't in question.

Laertes agrees, but is angry that his father's funeral was such a paltry affair.

So you shall. And where the offence is, let the great axe fall.

Claudius agrees. Laertes seems satisfied for the moment...

1. as mortal as: as vulnerable as.   2. If by . . . touched: If they decide that I was directly or indirectly involved.
3. obscure funeral: secret funeral, without proper ceremony.

Hamlet's Escape

Messengers bring Horatio a letter from Hamlet.

Hamlet tells how he escaped the ship to England.

and in the grapple I boarded them. On the instant they got clear of our ship, so I alone became their prisoner.

The pirates let Hamlet go because they had an errand for him.

Meanwhile, in the king's chamber, Claudius tells Laertes that Hamlet tried to kill him too.

He invents reasons for not bringing Hamlet to justice.

Laertes believes him, and wants revenge – exactly as Claudius planned.

Claudius receives Hamlet's letter.

---

1. of very warlike appointment: very aggressive, as if at war.   2. pursued my life: tried to kill me.   3. proceeded not: took no action.   4. general gender: common people.   5. desperate terms: an extreme or hopeless state.

But let him come. It warms the very sickness in my heart that I shall live and tell him to his teeth, 'Thus diest thou.'

Laertes welcomes the confrontation.

Laertes, was your father dear to you?

Why ask you this?

Hamlet comes back. What would you undertake to show yourself in deed your father's son more than in words?

To cut his throat in the church.

Claudius goads Laertes, trying to make him angrier still.

A fencing match is to be arranged, and Laertes will have a sharpened blade.

He, being remiss[1]... and free from all contriving, will not peruse the foils.[2]

Laertes will poison the point of his rapier.

I'll touch my point with this contagion.[3]

Claudius plans to have a poisoned cup at the ready, too.

A chalice[4]... whereon but sipping...

One woe doth tread upon another's heel,[5] so fast they follow. Your sister's drowned, Laertes.

Gertrude brings news of yet another tragedy: Ophelia is dead.

How much I had to do to calm his rage!

Now fear I this will give it start again.

Laertes is in despair. Claudius' plotting may not have been necessary.

1. remiss: trusting.   2. peruse the foils: check the swords.   3. contagion: poison.   4. chalice: cup.
5. One woe . . . heel: One tragedy follows right after another.

A SECRET FUNERAL

Is she to be buried in Christian burial when she wilfully seeks her own salvation?[1]

The gravediggers aren't sure it's right to bury a suspected suicide in holy ground.

This might be the pate[2] of a politician, which this ass now o'erreaches.[3]

Hamlet contemplates the skulls.

Who is to be buried in't?

One that was a woman, sir, but rest her soul, she's dead.

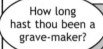

How long hast thou been a grave-maker?

I came to't...the very day that young Hamlet was born, he that is mad and sent into England.

Why was he sent to England?

He shall recover his wits there or, if he do not, it's no great matter there — there the men are as mad as he.

This same skull, sir, was Yorick's skull, the king's jester.

Alas, poor Yorick. I knew him, Horatio.

He hath borne me on his back a thousand times, and now how abhorred in my imagination it is![4]

Where be your gibes[5] now, your gambols, your songs?

Not one now to mock your own grinning?

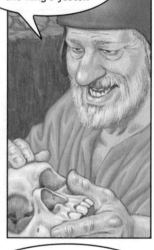

Now get you to my lady's chamber, and tell her, let her paint an inch thick, to this favour[6] she must come.

Make her laugh at that.

1. wilfully . . . salvation: takes her own life.   2. pate: head.
3. which . . . o'er-reaches: the gravedigger is now the superior of the politician.
4. borne . . . it is: he used to ride on the jester's back, but now the jester's skeleton horrifies him.   5. gibes: jokes.   6. this favour: the skull's appearance.

Here comes the king, the queen, the courtiers. Who is this they follow?

We should profane the service of the dead...

...to sing sage requiem.[2]

What ceremony else?[1]

Laertes is angry. There is to be no proper burial ceremony.

I tell thee, churlish priest, a ministering angel shall my sister be, when thou liest howling.[3]

What, the fair Ophelia!

Sweets to the sweet... I hoped thou shouldst have been my Hamlet's wife.

Hold off the earth awhile, till I have caught her once more in mine arms.

Laertes is overcome with emotion.

This is I, Hamlet the Dane.

The devil take thy soul!

Hamlet cannot restrain himself any longer.

I loved Ophelia. Forty thousand brothers could not with all their quantity of love make up my sum.

Good my lord, be quiet.

Pluck them asunder.[4]

Strengthen your patience in our last night's speech.[5]

1. What ceremony else?: Is this all there is to the funeral?   2. We should . . . reqiuem: We would be insulting the dead to mourn a suicide with a solemn burial service.   3. when thou liest howling: when you're screaming in hell.   4. Pluck them asunder: Pull them apart.   5. Strengthen . . . speech: Remember the plan we discussed last night, and be patient.

The Fencing Match

A courtier brings Laertes' challenge to Hamlet. To conceal his plot, the king has bet on Hamlet winning. Horatio is uneasy.

But Hamlet accepts the probability of death.

Hamlet scores the first hit.

Hamlet makes peace but Laertes insists on honour being satisfied.

The king toasts Hamlet and then offers him the poisoned cup.

Hamlet scores another hit. His mother is delighted. Claudius feigns pleasure.

Claudius is too late to stop the queen taking the poisoned cup.

1. forestall . . . hither: ask them not to come.   2. to come: in the future.
3. carouses to thy fortune: drinks to your health.

Have at you now!

Part them. They are incensed.[1]

Nay, come again.

They accidentally swap swords.

They bleed on both sides. How is it, my lord?

How is't, Laertes?

O my dear Hamlet! The drink, the drink! I am poisoned.

Laertes, mortally wounded, confesses his treachery.

Let the door be locked. Treachery! Seek it out.

Why, as a woodcock to mine own springe,[2] I am justly killed with mine own treachery.

Hamlet wounds Laertes.

It is here, Hamlet... The treacherous instrument is in thy hand.

The point envenomed[3] too! Then, venom, to thy work.

Here, thou incestuous,[4] murderous, damned Dane, drink off this potion... Follow my mother.

Exchange forgiveness with me,[5] noble Hamlet...

At last, Hamlet knows what to do. He stabs the king...

...and forces him to drink the rest of the poison.

Laertes' last act is to make peace with Hamlet.

1. incensed: seething with rage.   2. as a woodcock to mine own springe: caught in my own trap, like a foolish bird.
3. envenomed: poisoned.   4. incestuous: referring to the fact that Claudius married his brother's wife.
5. Exchange forgiveness with me: Forgive me as I forgive you.

AN HONOURABLE DEATH

> Horatio, I am dead, thou livest. Report me and my cause aright to the unsatisfied.[1]

Hamlet begs Horatio to explain to everyone what really happened.

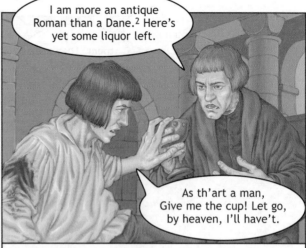

> I am more an antique Roman than a Dane.[2] Here's yet some liquor left.

> As th'art a man, Give me the cup! Let go, by heaven, I'll have't.

Horatio wants to die along with his friend, but Hamlet prevents him.

> O God, Horatio, what a wounded name. Things standing thus unknown, shall live behind me[3]...

> If thou didst ever hold me in thy heart, absent thee from felicity awhile,[4] and in this harsh world draw thy breath in pain, to tell my story.

Horatio must live to set the record straight, so that Hamlet is not dishonoured.

> Young Fortinbras, with conquest come from Poland, to the ambassadors of England gives this warlike volley.

There is gunfire outside.

Hamlet's last act is to approve the choice of Fortinbras as the new king of Denmark.

> I do prophesy th'election lights on Fortinbras...

> He has my dying voice[5]...

> Now cracks a noble heart. Good night, sweet prince...

> ...and flights of angels sing thee to thy rest.

1. Report . . . unsatisfied: Reveal the truth to those who do not know.   2. more . . . Dane: ancient Romans preferred suicide to dishonour.   3. what a . . . behind me: my name would be dishonoured if people in future times believed that I killed Claudius unjustly.   4. absent thee . . . awhile: put off the death you long for.   5. voice: vote. In death, Hamlet chooses Fortinbras to be the next king.

The Prince of Norway cannot believe his eyes – so many dead!

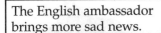
The English ambassador brings more sad news.

Rosencrantz and Guildenstern are dead.

Give order that these bodies high on a stage be placed to the view, and let me speak to th'yet unknowing world how these things came about.

Horatio volunteers to explain everything.

This is not how Fortinbras would have chosen to become king.

Let us haste to hear it... For me, with sorrow I embrace my fortune.

Bear Hamlet, like a soldier, to the stage. For he was likely, had he been put on,[2] to have proved most royal.

Hamlet's body is to be displayed ceremonially, like a hero's. He would have made a good soldier, and a good king.

Such a sight as this becomes the field, but here shows much amiss.[3] Go, bid the soldiers shoot.[4]

Death is expected on the battlefield, but in the royal palace it is a tragic sight.

1. what . . . cell: He imagines death feasting on the slain.   2. put on: put to the test.
3. shows much amiss: is out of place.   4. bid . . . shoot: fire the guns to salute Hamlet's death.

The end

Macbeth

William Shakespeare

Illustrated by
Nick Spender

Retold by
Stephen Haynes

Series created and designed by
David Salariya

When shall we three meet again,
in thunder, lightning, or in rain?

When the hurly-burly's done,
when the battle's lost and won.

That will be ere[1] the set of sun.

Fair is foul, and foul is fair:
hover through the fog and filthy air.

1. ere: before.

MAIN CHARACTERS

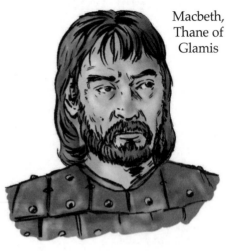

Macbeth,
Thane of
Glamis

Lady Macbeth

Banquo, a thane
of Scotland

Duncan,
King of Scotland

Malcolm,
Duncan's elder son

Donalbain,
Duncan's younger son

Macduff,
Thane of Fife

Lady Macduff

Lennox and Ross,
thanes of Scotland

Angus,
a thane of Scotland

The weird sisters

A NATIONAL HERO

Scotland, AD 1040.

The treacherous Macdonald has rebelled against King Duncan, the rightful king of Scotland. Duncan has sent his two most trusted generals, Macbeth and Banquo, to put down the rebellion.

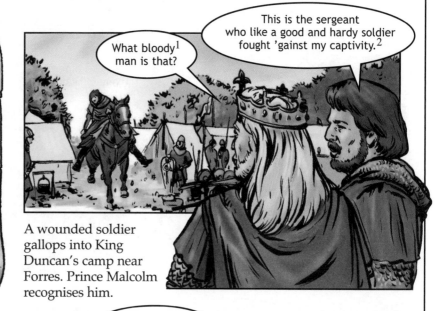

A wounded soldier gallops into King Duncan's camp near Forres. Prince Malcolm recognises him.

The sergeant describes how Macbeth fearlessly charged through the rebels, looking for their leader.

He slew Macdonald and stuck his head on the battlements as a warning to others.

No sooner had Macbeth defeated the rebels than the King of Norway[3] attacked from the other direction.

A Scottish nobleman, the Thane[4] of Cawdor, fought on the Norwegian side, but Macbeth eventually forced them to surrender.

Duncan is furious when he hears of Cawdor's treachery.

1. bloody: bloodstained.   2. 'gainst my captivity: to save me from being captured.   3. Norway: Some parts of Scotland are closer to Norway than they are to England, and raids were common.   4. Thane: a rank of the Scottish nobility, slightly below an English earl.   5. present: immediate.   6. with . . . Macbeth: Tell Macbeth that he is the new Thane of Cawdor.
7. hath: has.

A PROPHECY

The three weird sisters[3] prepare to waylay Macbeth and Banquo as they return from their victorious campaign.

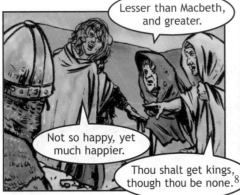

Macbeth wants to know more.

What can this mean? Banquo asks whether the sisters have any message for him. They answer him with riddles.

But instead of answering him, the witches vanish. Macbeth and Banquo can scarcely believe what they have heard.

The Thanes of Ross and Angus come riding to meet Macbeth with a message from the king.

Angus explains that Cawdor has been sentenced to death, and his title has been given to Macbeth. Does this mean that the other prophecies might also come true?

---

1. hast thou: have you.   2. doth come: is coming.   3. weird sisters: witches. 'Weird' means 'to do with fate or destiny'.
4. Hail to thee: Greetings to you.   5. Glamis: usually pronounced 'glahmz'.   6. shalt: shall   7. hereafter: afterwards.
8. Thou . . . none: You will have children who are kings, but you will not be one yourself.   9. stands . . . belief: is totally
unbelievable.   10. went it not so?: isn't that what they said?   11. thy: your.   12. bade me: told me to ('bade' is usually
pronounced 'bad').   13. thee: you.   14. behind: still to come.

46

Why do I yield to that suggestion whose horrid image doth unfix my hair?[1]

If chance will have me king, why, chance may crown me, without my stir.[2]

Very frankly he confessed his treasons, implored your highness' pardon, and set forth a deep repentance.

Back at King Duncan's camp

Banquo warns him that the witches are messengers of the devil and cannot be trusted. But Macbeth is not listening. He *could* become king, if he dared... Or perhaps, if he is fated to be king, it will somehow just happen by itself?

Prince Malcolm reports to his father that the traitor Cawdor has been executed.

O worthiest cousin! More is thy due[5] than more than all can pay.

There's no art to find the mind's construction in the face.[4]

Nothing in his life became him[3] like the leaving it.

He was a gentleman on whom I built an absolute trust.

The heroes return, and the king congratulates them.
But now Duncan has a most important announcement to make.

We will establish our estate upon our eldest, Malcolm, whom we name hereafter the Prince of Cumberland.[6]

That is a step on which I must fall down, or else o'erleap,[7] for in my way it lies.

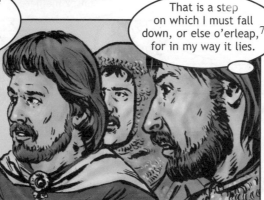

Stars, hide your fires; let not light see my black and deep desires.

He has decided who should succeed him as King of Scots.

Macbeth is dismayed: this means that Malcolm, not Macbeth, is now the heir to the throne.

If he really wants to be king, he will have to seize the crown for himself.

1. unfix my hair: make my hair stand on end.   2. without my stir: without my doing anything.   3. became him: was worthy of him. In other words, his death was the most noble act of his whole life.   4. There's . . . face: There is no way to judge a person's character from their appearance.   5. More is thy due: You deserve more.   6. Prince of Cumberland: the title of the heir to the Scottish throne.   7. a step . . . o'erleap: an obstacle that will stop me unless I can get over it.

AMBITION

'My dearest partner of greatness!'

Macbeth's castle at Inverness

Glamis thou art,[1] and Cawdor; and shalt be what thou art promised.

Yet do I fear thy nature: it is too full o'th'milk of human kindness.

Macbeth has written to his wife about the witches' prophecy and his new appointment as Thane of Cawdor.

She is thrilled by the news.

But will Macbeth be ruthless enough to make sure that the prophecy comes true?

Hie thee hither,[2] that I may pour my spirits in thine ear,

and chastise with the valour of my tongue all that impedes thee from the golden round.[3]

It will be up to her to make sure that he is!

The king comes here tonight.

Thou'rt mad to say it![4]

So please you, it is true.

A servant brings the news that Duncan is on his way to Inverness.

The raven himself is hoarse that croaks the fatal entrance of Duncan under my battlements.

Come, you spirits that tend on mortal thoughts,[5] unsex me here,[6]

and fill me from the crown to the toe top-full of direst cruelty!

So her chance has come already! Duncan will be here, in her own house, at her mercy.

She must steel herself, and put any thought of pity out of her mind.

1. thou art: you are.   2. hie thee hither: hurry here.   3. chastise . . . round: persuade you to ignore the doubts that keep you from seizing the crown.   4. Thou'rt mad to say it!: Why is she so startled? Does she think for a moment that when the servant says 'the king' he means Macbeth? Or does she find it hard to believe that Duncan has already fallen into her hands?   5. tend on mortal thoughts: encourage thoughts of death.   6. unsex me: make me forget that I am a woman; make me as ruthless as a man.

At last Macbeth himself arrives. She greets
him by his new title for the first time.

They both have the same thought:
Duncan must die.

They must welcome Duncan graciously
and behave as though all is well. He will
suspect nothing.

1. goes hence: goes away – but it can also mean 'dies'.   2. purposes: intends.   3. put . . . into my dispatch: let me
organise it.   4. look up clear: look cheerful.   5. to alter . . . fear: changing your expression is always a sign that
you are afraid.

A ROYAL VISIT

King Duncan and his lords approach Macbeth's castle. They are charmed by the delightful, peaceful scene.

Lady Macbeth comes out to welcome them, curtseying graciously.

A magnificent feast has been prepared for the royal guest, but Macbeth has left the hall to be alone for a while. He is getting cold feet.

There are good reasons why he should not kill Duncan.

In fact, it is Macbeth's duty to protect his guest.

Lady Macbeth has come to find him. He should be entertaining his royal visitor, not skulking in the dark by himself.

Macbeth has finally made up his mind.

1. seat: location.   2. we are: I am. It was usual for kings and queens to call themselves 'we'; later, Macbeth will do the same.   3. If . . . done: If it could all be safely over and done with.   4. 'twere well: it would be a good thing.   5. kinsman: relative (Macbeth and Duncan are cousins).   6. I have . . . itself: The only thing that drives me on (as a spur drives a horse) is ambition, which makes me attempt too much.   7. supped: finished eating.

But Lady Macbeth has laid her plans and will not stop now. Where is his courage?

She would not give up so easily. She would murder her own baby, if she had to!

Now she tries to flatter him.

Her plan is to get Duncan's servants drunk, and use their daggers to kill him.

1. Was the hope . . . freely?: She compares him to a man who is brave when he is drunk, but not when he wakes up the next morning.   2. such . . . love: this is what I think your love for me is worth.   3. Prithee: I beg you.   4. become a man: be worthy of a man.   5. who dares . . . none: anyone who does what is unworthy of a man is not a man.   6. durst: dared.   7. screw . . . sticking-place: summon all your courage (like winding a crossbow as tight as it will go).   8. received: believed by everyone.   9. done't: done it.   10. mock . . . show: trick everyone by pretending that all is well.

THE GHOSTLY DAGGER

What, sir, not yet at rest? The king's abed.

Late that night, in Macbeth's castle

This diamond he greets your wife withal,[1] by the name of most kind hostess.

Banquo and his son Fleance are on their way to bed when they hear footsteps in the dark. Alarmed, Banquo draws his sword – but it is only Macbeth.

The king has entrusted Banquo with a valuable gift for Lady Macbeth

I dreamed last night of the three weird sisters; to you they have showed some truth.

Macbeth pretends he has forgotten about the prophecies. They both know this is not true.

I think not of them.

Yet, when we can entreat an hour to serve,[2] we would spend it in some words upon that business – if you would grant the time.

Good repose the while.[3]

Thanks, sir; the like[4] to you.

Macbeth bids Banquo and Fleance goodnight.

Go bid thy mistress, when my drink is ready, she strike upon the bell. Get thee to bed.

Macbeth has arranged for his wife to give a secret signal as soon as the servants are unconscious.

1. withal: with.   2. when we can entreat an hour to serve: when I have time to spare. Macbeth is already using the 'royal plural' – saying 'we' when he means 'I'.   3. the while: meanwhile.   4. the like: the same.

Is this a dagger which I see before me, the handle toward my hand?

I have thee not, and yet I see thee still.

Art thou but a dagger of the mind?

I see thee still, and on thy blade and dudgeon[1] gouts[2] of blood, which was not so before.

Left alone in the darkened castle, Macbeth is suddenly confronted with a ghostly apparition.

He tries to take hold of it but his hand goes straight through.

It seems to be leading him towards Duncan's bedchamber. As he follows it, he sees drops of blood glistening on it.

There's no such thing: it is the bloody business which informs thus to mine eyes.[3]

Thou sure and firm-set earth, hear not my steps, which way they walk, for fear thy very stones[4] prate[5] of my whereabout.

He rubs his eyes, and the dagger vanishes.

He treads as quietly as he can, afraid that any sound on the flagstones may give him away.

I go, and it is done;[6] the bell invites me.

TING!

Behind him, the bell rings quietly, as planned.

Hear it not, Duncan; for it is a knell[7] that summons thee to heaven or to hell.

1. dudgeon: handle.   2. gouts: drops   3. it is . . . eyes: the thought of murder is making me see things that are not real.   4. thy very stones: even your stones.   5. prate: tell tales.   6. I go . . . done: As soon as I go, it will be over and done with.   7. knell: funeral bell.

THE DEED IS DONE

He is about it.[1]

Who's there? What ho!

Alack,[2] I am afraid they have awaked, and 'tis[3] not done.

I laid their daggers ready; he could not miss 'em.

Lady Macbeth is waiting for her husband to come back after killing Duncan. The suspense is unbearable; the slightest noise alarms her. A voice calls out in a distant corridor. Who can it be?

She has drugged the servants and put their daggers where Macbeth could find them – what could go wrong?

Had he not resembled my father as he slept, I had done't.[4]

Only one thing stopped her from killing Duncan herself.

My husband?

The door creaks open.

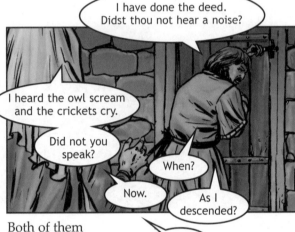

I have done the deed. Didst thou not hear a noise?

I heard the owl scream and the crickets cry.

Did not you speak?

When?

Now.

As I descended?

Ay.[5]

Both of them are on edge.

This is a sorry sight.

A foolish thought, to say a sorry sight.

Macbeth has blood on his hands.

Methought[6] I heard a voice cry, 'Sleep no more; Macbeth does murder sleep' –

– the innocent sleep, sleep that knits up the ravelled sleeve of care.[7]

Go get some water, and wash this filthy witness[8] from your hand.

Somewhere in the castle, he heard someone wake.

Lady Macbeth has no time for this nonsense.

1. He is about it: He is doing it now. 2. alack: alas. 3. 'tis: it is. 4. I had done't: I would have done it. 5. Ay: yes.
6. methought: it seemed to me. 7. knits . . . care: cures us of our everyday worries, as if it was mending a frayed
garment. 8. witness: evidence.

Why did you bring these daggers from the place? They must lie there.

Go carry them; and smear the sleepy grooms with blood.

I'll go no more. I am afraid to think what I have done; look on't again I dare not.

Infirm of purpose![1] Give *me* the daggers.

The sleeping and the dead are but as pictures;[2] 'tis the eye of childhood that fears a painted devil.[3]

She suddenly notices that Macbeth is still carrying the servants' daggers. He was supposed to leave them as incriminating evidence!

KNOCK! KNOCK!

Whence[4] is that knocking?

How is't with me,[5] when every noise appals[6] me?

Will all great Neptune's[7] ocean wash this blood clean from my hand?

As Lady Macbeth goes to return the daggers, there is a loud knocking at the castle gate.

KNOCK! KNOCK!

KNOCK! KNOCK!

Retire we to our chamber; a little water clears us of this deed.

Wake Duncan with thy knocking! I would thou couldst![10]

No, this my hand will rather the multitudinous[8] seas incarnadine,[9] making the green one red.

Lady Macbeth has returned from planting the daggers.

1. Infirm of purpose: indecisive, easily discouraged.   2. but as pictures: only like pictures.   3. 'tis . . . devil: only children are afraid of a picture of something frightening.   4. whence: from where.   5. How is't with me?: What's the matter with me?   6. appals: frightens.   7. Neptune: Roman god of the sea.   8. multitudinous: many, vast.   9. incarnadine: stain red
10. I would thou couldst: I wish you could.

O Horror, Horror, Horror!

The south gate of the castle; dawn

KNOCK! KNOCK!

Anon, anon![3] I pray you, remember the porter.

KNOCK! KNOCK!

Here's a knocking indeed! If a man were porter[1] of hell-gate, he should have old[2] turning the key.

Is thy master stirring?[4]

The gatekeeper finally arrives to see who is knocking. He has enjoyed the feast, and had far too much to drink.

Is the king stirring, worthy thane?

Not yet.

He did command me to call timely[5] on him.

Our chimneys were blown down; and, as they say, lamentings heard i'th'air[6] — strange screams of death.

'Twas[7] a rough night.

O HORROR, HORROR, HORROR!

Macduff and Lennox have arrived early to call on the king. As they step through the gate, Macbeth comes to meet them, pulling his cloak around him to make them think he has just woken up.

While Macduff goes to see the king, Lennox tells Macbeth that he and Macduff have not slept well. But then a sudden shout rings through the castle.

Confusion now hath made his masterpiece! Most sacrilegious[8] murder!

Mean you his majesty?

Do not bid me[9] speak; see, and then speak yourselves.

Awake, awake! Ring the alarum-bell![10] Murder and treason!

Our royal master's murdered!

What, in our house?

Macduff comes rushing back from the king's chamber with the most dreadful news.

Macbeth and Lennox rush off to see for themselves, while Macduff rouses the whole household. Lady Macbeth and Banquo are the first to arrive.

1. porter: gatekeeper   2. old: a lot of.   3. anon: soon (in other words, 'I'm coming!').   4. stirring: awake.
5. timely: early.   6. i'th': in the.   7. 'twas: it was.   8. sacrilegious: hateful to God. (In Shakespeare's time it was believed that kings were chosen by God.)   9. bid me: ask me to.   10. alarum: alarm.

Those of his chamber, as it seemed, had done't.

Your royal father's murdered.

O, yet I do repent me of my fury, that I did kill them.

Wherefore[1] did you so?

Who can be wise, amazed, temp'rate[2] and furious, loyal and neutral, in a moment? No man.[3]

Help me hence, ho!

Look to the lady.

Is't known who did this more than bloody[5] deed?

Those that Macbeth hath slain.

Macduff breaks the news to Duncan's sons, Malcolm and Donalbain. Lennox, having examined the crime scene, is convinced by Macbeth's alibi.

While Macbeth struggles to answer Macduff's awkward question, Lady Macbeth creates a diversion by pretending to feel faint.

Where we are, there's daggers in men's smiles.

And Duncan's horses — a thing most strange and certain — turned wild in nature.

'Tis said they eat[4] each other.

They did so.

Duncan's sons are afraid that they will be killed next. They decide to flee.

Later that day, as Macduff is leaving the castle, he finds Ross and an old man discussing the strange omens that have been reported.

The king's two sons are stol'n away and fled, which puts upon them suspicion of the deed.

Then 'tis most like[6] the sovereignty[7] will fall upon Macbeth.

He is already named, and gone to Scone[8] to be invested.[9]

Will you to[10] Scone?

No, cousin, I'll to Fife.

God's benison[11] go with you.

But now the sudden departure of Malcolm and Donalbain has given Macbeth a further alibi.

Macduff has decided not to attend Macbeth's coronation. He is going home instead.

1. wherefore: why.   2. temp'rate: temperate, calm.   3. Who . . . no man: When you are astonished and angry, you cannot behave wisely and calmly; if you are loyal to your king, you cannot forget your loyalty. Macbeth is pretending that he was so angry with the servants that he could not help killing them.   4.eat: ate.   5. bloody: bloodthirsty.   6. like: likely.
7. sovereignty: kingship.   8. Scone: the ancient capital of Scotland, where the King of Scots was traditionally crowned.
9. invested: made king in a special ceremony.   10. Will you to: Will you go to.   11. benison: blessing.

A Contract to Kill

...and I fear thou play'dst most foully for't.[1]

Thou hast it now: King, Cawdor, Glamis, all, as the weird women promised...

Macbeth and his lady have been crowned at Scone. The witches' prophecy to Macbeth has been fulfilled. Banquo is beginning to be suspicious.

Yet it was said... myself should be the root and father of many kings.

Here's our chief guest.

Tonight we hold a solemn supper, sir, and I'll request your presence.

But what of their prediction for Banquo – that his descendants will inherit the throne?

Macbeth is planning a grand feast to celebrate his coronation, and Banquo is to be the guest of honour.

Ride you this afternoon?

Fail not[2] our feast.

We hear our bloody cousins are bestowed[3] in England and in Ireland, not confessing their cruel parricide,[4] filling their hearers with strange invention.[5]

Ay, my good lord.

My lord, I will not.

But first Banquo has a journey to make.

The official story now is that Malcolm and Donalbain are the killers.

1. play'dst . . . for't: got it by unfair means.   2. fail not: do not miss.   3. bestowed: hidden away.
4. parricide: the murder of their own father.   5. strange invention: made-up stories. (No doubt they are telling people that Macbeth is the murderer.)

Banquo and his young son mount their horses.

Macbeth realises that Banquo has behaved more wisely than he has.

And he has not forgotten the prediction about Banquo's children.

He has arranged a secret meeting with two desperate characters.

He wants Banquo killed, but it must be done secretly. Fleance must die too.

1. To be . . . safely thus: It is no use being king unless you are safely king.   2. rubs nor botches: mistakes.
3. thy soul's . . . tonight: If heaven is where your soul is going, it will go there tonight.

A Botched Job

King Macbeth and his queen are not enjoying their new status at all. They live in constant fear, and are tormented by nightmares.

Duncan is better off than they are – he no longer has anything to worry about.

But Macbeth's plan is underway...

---

1. Nought's had . . . content: When we get what we wanted and are still not happy, we have gained nothing for our trouble.   2. Things . . . regard: There is no point worrying about things that cannot be changed.   3. let . . . disjoint: let the whole world fall apart.   4. both the worlds: heaven and earth.   5. ere: before, rather than.   6. Be innocent . . . deed: You had better not know about it yet, but you will be pleased once it is done.

Light thickens,
and the crow makes wing[1] to th'rooky wood;
good things of day begin to droop and drowse,
while night's black agents to their preys do rouse.[2]

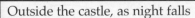

Outside the castle, as night falls

Hark! I hear horses.

It will be rain tonight.

Let it come down!

The two murderers lie in wait for Banquo and Fleance as they return to the castle. Macbeth has sent a third man to give them their instructions – and perhaps to keep an eye on them as well.

Banquo and Fleance, suspecting nothing, dismount from their horses to walk to the castle gate.

O, treachery!
Fly, good Fleance, fly, fly, fly!
Thou mayst revenge.

Who did strike out the light?

Was't not the way?[3]

There's but one down;[4] the son is fled.

1. makes wing: flies.　2. rouse: awake.　3. Was't . . . way?: Wasn't that the plan?　4. but one down: only one killed.

Banquo Returns

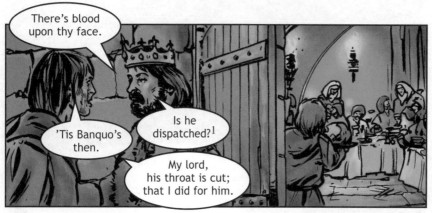

The new king and queen have put on a splendid banquet for the Scottish noblemen. But Macbeth is not at the table; he has spotted one of the murderers lurking in the shadows by the door.

But the murder has not gone according to plan.

Fleance will be dangerous one day – and his descendants could be kings!

Lady Macbeth has called him back to the feast.

But when Macbeth goes to sit down, he finds his seat taken! Banquo has come to the feast after all – just as he promised.

1. dispatched: got rid of.   2. venom: poison. Once he is grown up, Fleance will be as dangerous to Macbeth as a poisonous snake, because he will want revenge.   3. gory locks: bloodstained hair.

Gentlemen, rise: his highness is not well.

Sit, worthy friends. My lord is often thus.[1] Upon a thought[2] he will again be well.

The guests do not know what to think; they cannot see what Macbeth is staring at.

Are you a man?

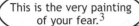

This is the very painting of your fear.[3]

This is the air-drawn dagger which — *you said* — led you to Duncan.

The ghost has vanished.

Why do you make such faces? When all's done, you look but on[4] a stool.

Now that the ghost has gone, Macbeth pulls himself together and proposes a toast.

I drink to th'general joy o'th'whole table, and to our dear friend Banquo, whom we miss. Would[5] he were here!

Avaunt,[6] and quit my sight! Let the earth hide thee!

But as soon as Banquo's name is mentioned, the ghost reappears. Lady Macbeth has to send the guests away.

He grows worse and worse.

At once, good night. Stand not upon the order of your going,[7] but go at once.

1. thus: like this.   2. upon a thought: in no time at all.   3. painting of your fear: hallucination caused by fear.
4. you look but on: you are only looking at.   5. would: I wish.   6. Avaunt: Go away.   7. Stand . . . going: Don't insist on leaving in the proper order (with the most important people going first).

STIRRINGS OF REBELLION

It will have blood; they say blood will have blood.

The embarrassed guests have gone, leaving Macbeth and his Lady alone.

How sayst thou, that Macduff denies his person[1] at our great bidding?

Did you send to him,[2] sir?

I hear it by the way, but I will send.

Macduff was invited to the feast; why didn't he come?

There's not a one of them but in his house I keep a servant fee'd.[3]

Macbeth has spies everywhere; he no longer trusts anyone.

I will tomorrow – and betimes[4] I will – to the weird sisters. More shall they speak.

He wants no more uncertainty. He has resolved to find out the worst – by confronting the three sisters once more.

I am in blood stepped in so far that, should I wade no more, returning were[5] as tedious as go o'er.

We are yet but young in deed.[6]

Now that he has so many deaths on his conscience, there is no turning back.

Meanwhile, in a secret place...

How did you dare to trade and traffic[7] with Macbeth in riddles and affairs of death?

Hecate, goddess of sorcery, is angry with the weird sisters. They should have consulted her before meddling with Macbeth's destiny.

He shall spurn[8] fate, scorn death, and bear his hopes 'bove wisdom, grace and fear.

And you all know, security[9] is mortals' chiefest enemy.

They must encourage Macbeth in his evil plans. In the end, he will go too far – and bring about his own destruction.

1. How . . . person: What do you think of the fact that Macduff refuses to come?   2. send to him: send a messenger to him (to find out why).   3. fee'd: paid.   4. betimes: early.   5. were: would be. Like a man wading through a river, he has gone so far that going back would be just as difficult as going on.   6. We are . . . deed: We still have much more to do/We are not yet used to doing these things.   7. traffic: deal.   8. spurn: scorn.   9. security: thinking you are safe.

Things have been strangely borne.[1] The gracious Duncan was pitied of Macbeth — marry,[2] he was dead.

Meanwhile, far from Macbeth's castle...

Lennox and another lord are discussing the sorry state that Scotland is in now that Macbeth has become king. Everyone knows who is responsible for the mysterious deaths, but no-one dares to say so.

And the right-valiant Banquo walked too late; whom you may say, if't please you, Fleance killed, for Fleance fled.

Men must not walk too late.

Some people pretend to think that Fleance killed Banquo and ran away.

How it did grieve Macbeth! Did he not straight[4] in pious[5] rage the two delinquents tear?

Who cannot want the thought[3] how monstrous it was for Malcolm and for Donalbain to kill their gracious father?

Was not that nobly done?

Others say that Malcolm and Donalbain killed their own father. Or is it the two murdered servants who are supposed to be guilty?

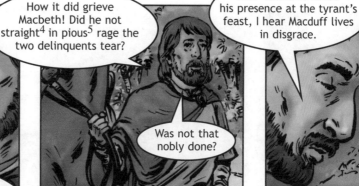

And 'cause he failed his presence at the tyrant's feast, I hear Macduff lives in disgrace.

And now Macduff is suspected because he refused to attend the feast.

I'll send my prayers with him.

The other lord has news of Macduff: he is in England, trying to persuade King Edward the Confessor and the Earl of Northumberland to fight against Macbeth.

1. borne: done, carried out.   2. marry: a mild oath.   3. Who . . . thought: Everyone is bound to think.
4. straight: straight away.   5. pious: virtuous.

A Vision of the Future

Hecate looks on as the weird sisters brew their gruesome potion.

Thrice the brindled[1] cat hath mewed.

Harpier[3] cries, ''Tis time, 'tis time!'

Thrice and once the hedge-pig[2] whined.

Double, double toil and trouble; fire burn and cauldron bubble!

Fillet of a fenny[4] snake, in the cauldron boil and bake; eye of newt and toe of frog, wool of bat and tongue of dog.

Double, double toil and trouble; fire burn and cauldron bubble!

By the pricking of my thumbs, something wicked this way comes.[5]

How now, you secret, black, and midnight hags! What is't you do?

A deed without a name.

Macbeth has come to find out more about the future.

I conjure you,[6] by that which you profess,[7] howe'er you come to know it, answer me.

Say if thou'dst rather hear it from our mouths, or from our masters'.

Macbeth, Macbeth, Macbeth! Beware Macduff; beware the Thane of Fife.[8]

Macbeth, Macbeth, Macbeth! Be bloody,[9] bold, and resolute.[10]

Call 'em; let me see 'em.

Whate'er thou art, for thy good caution, thanks.

Laugh to scorn[11] the power of man, for none of woman born[12] shall harm Macbeth.

He demands to know the whole truth, come what may. He is not afraid to face any evil spirits.

Throwing more grisly ingredients into their cauldron, the witches conjure up a fearsome apparition.

As the first apparition vanishes, a second arises from the fuming cauldron.

1. brindled: with dark stripes. 2. hedge-pig: hedgehog. 3. Harpier: the name of an evil spirit. 4. fenny: from a marshy place. 5. By . . . comes: Macbeth is now so evil that even the witches feel their skin tingle when he is near. 6. conjure you: solemnly call upon you. 7. profess: believe in. 8. Thane of Fife: Macduff. 9. bloody: bloodthirsty. 10. resolute: firm. 11. laugh to scorn: think nothing of. 12. none of woman born: this usually means 'no mortal man'.

So Macbeth need fear no mortal man! But he will take no chances: Macduff must die.

A third apparition emerges.

But there is one more thing he must know.

1. issue: children, descendants. 2. crack of doom: end of the world.
3. blood-boltered: bloodstained.

A MASSACRE OF INNOCENTS

The witches and their apparitions vanish, and Macbeth is puzzled to find himself suddenly alone with the Thane of Lennox.

So Macbeth's suspicions are confirmed, and this time he will not hesitate: he will wipe out the entire family.

Macduff's castle in Fife

Ross has come to warn Lady Macduff that her husband has fled to England. She is shocked.

Did he go because he was afraid, or was it part of a plan?

Lady Macduff is outraged at the thought that her husband has deserted them.

But Ross believes that Macduff had good reasons for going to England.

1. Came they not by you?: Didn't they pass you?   2. trace him in his line: are descended from him.
3. when . . . traitors: even when we have done nothing wrong, people think we are traitors because we run away in fear.
4. wants: lacks.   5. diminutive: tiny.   6. her young ones in her nest: when she has her young ones in her nest.
7. judicious: able to make wise decisions.   8. the fits o'th'season: the way things are now.

The little boy is puzzled by all this talk of traitors.

They are interrupted by a messenger who rushes in unannounced.

There is no time to run: already Macbeth's henchmen are at the door.

1. that he was: in law, Macduff is a traitor because he is conspiring against his king; but Lady Macduff probably means that he has betrayed his family by leaving them behind.   2. swears: makes a promise on oath.   3. hence: away from here.   4. whither: where to.   5. fry: offspring.

THE NEXT KING OF SCOTLAND?

Meanwhile, in England:

This tyrant,[1] whose sole name blisters our tongues,[2] was once thought honest.

You have loved him well — he hath not touched you yet.[3]

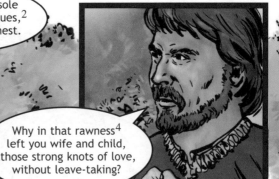

Why in that rawness[4] left you wife and child, those strong knots of love, without leave-taking?

Malcolm and Macduff are at the court of King Edward the Confessor – a man so saintly, they say, that he can heal the sick by touching them.

Malcolm is suspicious of Macduff because he fled Scotland so suddenly, leaving his wife and children behind.

Bleed, bleed, poor country! I would not be the villain that thou think'st.

When I shall tread upon the tyrant's head, or wear it on my sword, yet my poor country shall have more vices than it had before.

Not in the legions of horrid hell can come a devil more damned in evils to top Macbeth.

Macduff has no answer to this; he can only reply that he is loyal to Scotland.

Malcolm believes that both Scotland and England will support his claim to be king. But he has a terrible confession to make: he thinks he would be an even worse king than Macbeth. Macduff cannot believe this.

I grant him bloody[5]...

We have willing dames enough.

So Malcolm decides to confess everything to him.

Malcolm cannot stop chasing after women. Macduff says this is a shame – but many women would be happy to be loved by a king.

And he cannot control his greed. Macduff says this is worse; but Scotland is a rich country, and can cope with a greedy king.

1. tyrant: cruel ruler.   2. whose . . . tongues: whose name we hate to speak.
3. he hath not touched you yet: Neither of them know yet what has happened to Macduff's family.
4. in that rawness: without protection.   5. I grant him bloody: I agree that he is bloodthirsty.

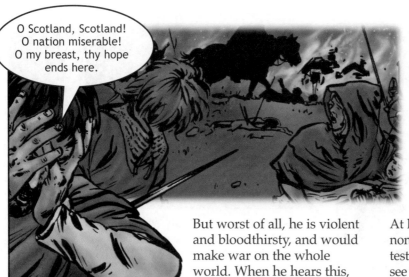

"O Scotland, Scotland! O nation miserable! O my breast, thy hope ends here."

"What I am truly is thine, and my poor country's, to command."

But worst of all, he is violent and bloodthirsty, and would make war on the whole world. When he hears this, Macduff is in despair.

At last Malcolm admits that none of this is true: he has been testing Macduff, and now he can see that Macduff has the good of Scotland at heart.

"Stands Scotland where it did?[1]"

"How does my wife?"

"Alas, poor country!"

"Why, well."

"And all my children?"

"Well, too."

"They were well at peace when I did leave 'em."

The Thane of Ross arrives with news from Scotland. But he cannot bear to tell Macduff the truth.

"Gracious England hath lent us good Siward and ten thousand men."

Malcolm tells Ross that the English have offered to help him defeat Macbeth.

"Your castle is surprised; your wife and babes savagely slaughtered."

"Merciful heaven!"

At last Ross summons up the courage to tell Macduff what has happened.

"All my pretty ones? Did you say all? What, all my pretty chickens and their dam[2] at one fell swoop?"

"Did heaven look on, and would not take their part?[3]"

"Within my sword's length set him; if he 'scape, heaven forgive him too."

He swears to fight for Malcolm and to kill Macbeth himself.

1. Stands . . . did?: Is Scotland still in the same state?   2. dam: mother.   3. take their part: be on their side.

CONSCIENCE

Macbeth's castle at Dunsinane

You see her eyes are open.

Ay, but their sense are shut.

For some time now, Lady Macbeth has been sleepwalking. One of her ladies in waiting is so alarmed that she has asked the doctor to come and see for himself.

Yet here's a spot. Out, damned spot! Out, I say!

Lady Macbeth goes through the motions of washing her hands. She has been doing this every night.

Fie, my lord, fie! A soldier, and afeard?[1]

Hell is murky.

What need we fear who knows it, when none can call our power to account?[2]

Again she scolds Macbeth for his lack of courage.

The Thane of Fife[3] had a wife. Where is she now? What, will these hands ne'er be clean?

Yet who would have thought the old man to have had so much blood in him?

She is reliving all their past crimes.

You have known what you should not.

She has spoke what she should not, I am sure of that. Heaven knows what she has known.

1. afeard: afraid.   2. none . . . account: there is no-one who can hold us responsible for what we have done.
3. Thane of Fife: Macduff.

She is beyond the doctor's help.

Near Birnam Wood

The thanes of Scotland are now in open rebellion against the tyrant Macbeth. They are on their way to Birnam Wood to meet the English army which has been sent to help them.

1. practice: professional skill or experience.   2. on's: of his.   3. More . . . physician: She needs a priest more than she needs a doctor.   4. power: army   5. well meet: welcome.

MACBETH STANDS ALONE

News has reached Macbeth that the Scottish thanes are moving against him.

Bring me no more reports; let them fly all.[1]

He remembers the witches' last two prophecies.

Till Birnam wood remove to Dunsinane, I cannot taint with[2] fear.

What's the boy Malcolm? Was he not born of woman?

A servant comes in with even more bad news. He is so afraid of Macbeth that he can hardly speak.

The devil damn thee black, thou cream-faced loon!

There is ten thousand...

Geese, villain?

...soldiers, sir.

Seyton![5]

I am sick at heart. I have lived long enough; my way of life is fall'n into the sere,[3] the yellow leaf;

and that which should accompany old age — as honour, love, obedience, troops of friends — I must not look[4] to have.

I'll fight till from my bones my flesh be hacked. Give me my armour.

Seyton, Macbeth's adjutant, arrives. The doctor has also been summoned.

How does your patient, doctor?

Not so sick, my lord, as she is troubled with thick-coming fancies[6] that keep her from her rest.

Cure her of that. Canst thou not minister[7] to a mind diseased, pluck from the memory a rooted sorrow?

Come, put mine armour on.

Throw physic[9] to the dogs; I'll none of it.[10]

Therein[8] the patient must minister to himself.

I will not be afraid of death and bane,[11] till Birnam forest come to Dunsinane.

---

1. let them fly all: I don't care if everyone deserts me.   2. taint with: be weakened by.   3. sere: withered.
4. look: expect.   5. Seyton: Some experts believe that this name was pronounced like 'Satan' in Shakespeare's time.
6. Not . . . fancies: She is not physically ill, but disturbed by wild imaginings which come one after the other.
7. minister: give medical treatment.   8. therein: in this kind of illness.   9. physic: medicine.   10. I'll none of it: I'll have nothing to do with it.   11. bane: destruction.

At Birnam Wood

Let every soldier hew him down a bough,[1] and bear't before him.

Malcolm, Macduff and Siward's English army arrive at Birnam Wood. Malcolm orders the soldiers to camouflage themselves with branches.

Back at Dunsinane

The queen, my lord, is dead.

She should have died hereafter; there would have been a time for such a word.

Tomorrow, and tomorrow, and tomorrow creeps in this petty pace[2] from day to day, to the last syllable of recorded time;

and all our yesterdays have lighted fools the way to dusty death.

Macbeth is getting the castle ready to withstand a siege, when he suddenly hears the wailing of women.

Out, out, brief candle!

Life's but a walking shadow, a poor player[3] that struts and frets[4] his hour upon the stage and then is heard no more.

It is a tale told by an idiot, full of sound and fury, signifying nothing.

As I did stand my watch upon the hill, I looked toward Birnam, and anon,[5] methought, the wood began to move.

Liar and slave!

A messenger arrives with news that is so bizarre, he hardly knows where to start.

Ring the alarum-bell![6] Blow wind, come wrack;[6] at least we'll die with harness[7] on our back.

1. hew . . . bough: cut down a branch for himself.   2. in this petty pace: slowly, step by step. He is saying that the future will trickle away as uselessly as the past.   3. player: actor.   4. frets: worries, fusses.   5. anon: presently, after a while.   6. wrack: destruction.   7. harness: armour.

DEATH OF A TYRANT

The army approaches Dunsinane.

Now near enough; your leafy screens throw down.

Make all our trumpets speak; give them all breath, those clamorous harbingers[1] of blood and death.

What is thy name?

Thou'lt be afraid to hear it.

Young Siward, the Earl of Northumberland's son, is the first to confront Macbeth.

My name's Macbeth.

The devil himself could not pronounce a title more hateful to mine ear.

Thou wast born of woman.

Tyrant, show thy face!

If thou be'st slain, and with no stroke of mine,[2] my wife and children's ghosts will haunt me still.[3]

Macbeth easily kills the inexperienced young warrior.

Macduff is determined to kill Macbeth himself. He will not fight anyone else.

Of all men else I have avoided thee.

Turn, hell-hound, turn!

At last he finds the man he has been seeking.

But get thee back — my soul is too much charged[4] with blood of thine already.

I have no words. My voice is in my sword, thou bloodier villain than terms can give thee out.[5]

Thou losest labour.[6] I bear a charmèd[7] life, which must not yield[8] to one of woman born.

1. clamorous harbingers: noisy messengers.   2. If . . . mine: If you are killed by anyone other than me.   3. still: always, for ever.   4. charged: burdened.   5. bloodier . . . than terms can give thee out: more bloodthirsty than words can say.
6. Thou losest labour: You're wasting your time.   7. charmèd: protected by magic.   8. yield: give way.

Despair thy charm — Macduff was from his mother's womb untimely[1] ripped.

I'll not fight with thee.

Then yield thee, coward, and live to be the show and gaze o'th'time.[2]

We'll have thee, as our rarer monsters are, painted on a pole, and underwrit,[3] 'Here may you see the tyrant.'

I will try the last.

Lay on, Macduff, and damned be him that first cries, 'Hold, enough!'[4]

The courtyard of the castle

Had he his hurts before?[5]

Ay, on the front.

Had I as many sons as I have hairs, I would not wish them to a fairer death.

The battle is over, and the castle has surrendered without a fight. Only now does Siward learn that his son is dead.

Behold where stands th'usurper's[6] cursèd head. The time is free.[7]

Hail, king — for so thou art.

Macduff presents Malcolm with a grisly trophy.

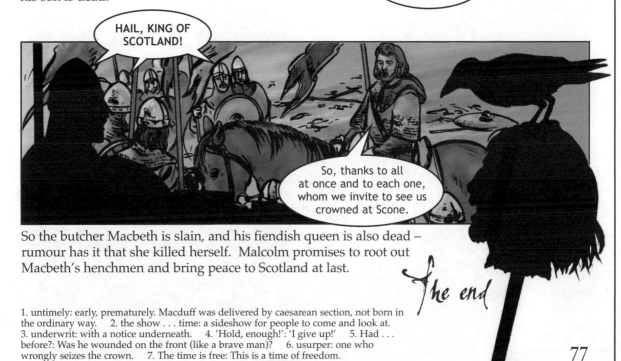

HAIL, KING OF SCOTLAND!

So, thanks to all at once and to each one, whom we invite to see us crowned at Scone.

So the butcher Macbeth is slain, and his fiendish queen is also dead – rumour has it that she killed herself. Malcolm promises to root out Macbeth's henchmen and bring peace to Scotland at last.

The end

1. untimely: early, prematurely. Macduff was delivered by caesarean section, not born in the ordinary way.   2. the show . . . time: a sideshow for people to come and look at.
3. underwrit: with a notice underneath.   4. 'Hold, enough!': 'I give up!'   5. Had . . . before?: Was he wounded on the front (like a brave man)?   6. usurper: one who wrongly seizes the crown.   7. The time is free: This is a time of freedom.

JULIUS
CAESAR

William Shakespeare

Illustrated by

Li Sidong

Retold by

Michael Ford

Series created and designed by

David Salariya

MAIN CHARACTERS

Brutus,
a senator

Julius Caesar,
consul of Rome

Mark Antony,
a senator

Portia, wife
of Brutus

Calpurnia,
wife of Caesar

Cassius,
a senator

Casca,
a tribune

Cicero, a
senator

Octavius Caesar, nephew
to Julius Caesar

Cinna the poet

Flavius and Marullus,
tribunes

A soothsayer

A Hero's Return?

Rome, 44 BC.

On the Feast of Lupercalia, citizens fill the streets to celebrate Julius Caesar's triumphant return to Rome. Four years ago, Caesar defeated his former friend Pompey the Great in a civil war. Now he has beaten Pompey's sons as well.

The tribunes[1] Marullus and Flavius are trying to make their way through the crowded streets.

Hence! Home, you idle creatures, get you home! Is this a holiday?

Speak, what trade art thou?[2]

A carpenter.

You, sir. What trade are you?

I am but, as you would say, a cobbler.

We make holiday to see Caesar and to rejoice in his triumph.[3]

Wherefore[4] rejoice? What conquest brings he home?

Marullus asks why everyone is outdoors and not working.

O you hard hearts, you cruel men of Rome. Knew you not Pompey?

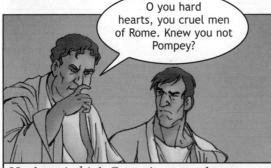

He doesn't think Caesar's return deserves such celebration. The consul[5] Pompey did much more for Rome.

Disrobe the images,[6] if you do find them decked with ceremonies.[7]

Flavius tells Marullus to try and calm the people, and to take down any decorations they have put up around the city.

1. tribune: a magistrate elected by the people. 2. art thou?: are you? 3. triumph: a grand procession to welcome a returning hero. 4. wherefore: why. 5. consul: the highest position in the Roman Senate. 6. images: statues of Caesar. 7. decked with ceremonies: decorated.

THE BEGINNINGS OF REVOLT

Caesar's procession makes its way through the streets towards the Palatine Hill[1] while the people celebrate.

Forget not in your speed, Antonio, to touch Calpurnia...

The barren,[2] touched in this holy chase,[3] shake off their sterile[4] curse.

Beware the Ides of March![5]

Caesar has no heir, because his wife Calpurnia can't have children. He reminds his general and friend, Mark Antony, of a Roman superstition about this.

A soothsayer[6] calls out to Caesar as he passes.

He is a dreamer, let us leave him.

The man is brought before Caesar, who dismisses his warning.

1. Palatine Hill: one of seven small hills on which the city of Rome was built. It is one of the most ancient parts of the city.   2. barren: unable to produce children.
3. holy chase: sacred procession.   4. sterile: means the same as 'barren'.   5. Ides of March: the 15th of March.
6. soothsayer: a person who claims to foretell the future.

Once Caesar and his followers have passed by, the senators[1] Cassius and Brutus remain.

Will you go see the order of the course?[2]

I am not gamesome.[3]

I do lack some part of that quick spirit[4] that is in Antony.

I turn the trouble of my countenance merely upon myself.[6]

If I have veiled my look[5]...

What means this shouting?

I do fear the people choose Caesar for their king.

Cassius asks Brutus, his brother-in-law, what is the matter.

Cassius says the people of Rome love Brutus. Brutus is suspicious of his flattery. They hear shouts.

Cassius tests Brutus' loyalty to Caesar. He hopes Brutus will join his plot to get rid of Caesar.

Cassius tells how he once saved Caesar from drowning and how fever turned this 'god' into a coward.

Ay, do you fear it?

Then must I think you would not have it so.

Once, upon a raw and gusty day...

...'tis true, this god did shake.

The fault, dear Brutus, is not in our stars...

What you would work me to, I have some aim.[7]

but in ourselves.

Casca brings news that Caesar was offered the crown, but refused it.

Well, Brutus, thou art noble...

The common herd was glad.[8]

Yet, I see, thy honourable mettle may be wrought from that it is disposed.[9]

He suggests that they are to blame for Caesar's fame.

The men arrange to meet the next night, and Cassius is left alone.

1. senators: members of the Senate, the governing body of ancient Rome. 2. the order of the course: the rest of the procession.
3. gamesome: fun-loving. 4. quick spirit: enthusiasm. 5. veiled my look: frowned. 6. I turn . . . myself: I'm thinking about my own problems. 7. What you . . . aim: I know what you're trying to make me do. 8. The common herd was glad: The common folk were cheering (because this act further convinces the people that Caesar is noble).
9. thy honourable . . . disposed: though you are honourable, it is possible to persuade you.

OMENS FROM THE HEAVENS

That night, thunder and lightning crash across the city.

Good even,[1] Casca.

Why are you breathless, and why stare you so?

Casca rushes into the street, pale with fear. Cicero spots him.

Either there is a civil strife in heaven[2]...

...or else the world, too saucy[3] with the gods, incenses[4] them to send destruction.

Casca says he has seen many terrifying things tonight. The gods must be angry.

He's seen a slave with his hands on fire, and he met a lion by the Capitol.[5]

Yesterday he heard there were men walking down the streets on fire...

...and an owl had sat screeching in the marketplace in broad daylight.

1. even: evening.   2. civil strife in heaven: war between the gods.   3. saucy: insolent, rude.
4. incenses: angers.   5. Capitol: another of the seven hills of Rome, site of the temple of Jupiter and the ancient citadel.

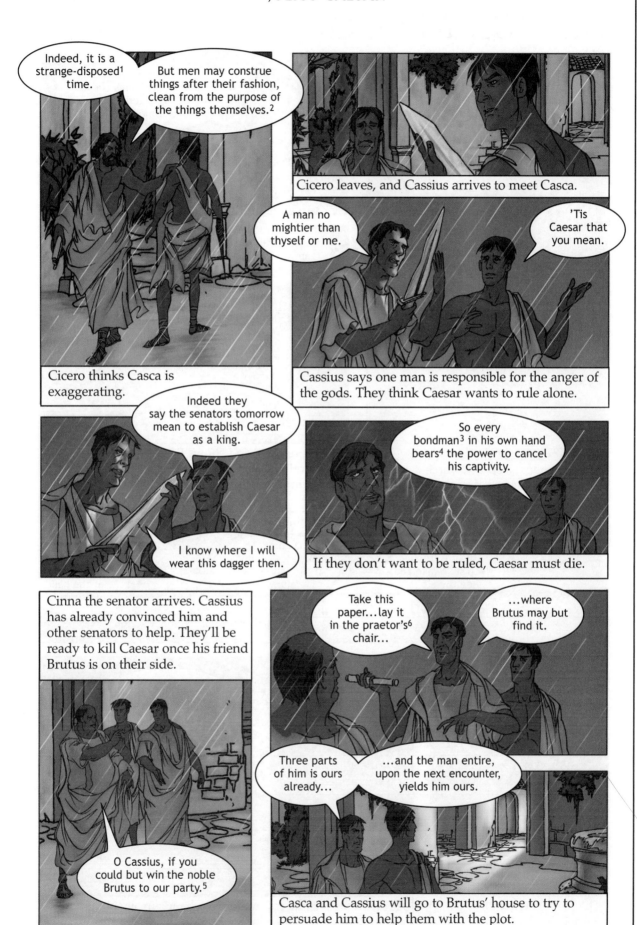

Indeed, it is a strange-disposed[1] time.

But men may construe things after their fashion, clean from the purpose of the things themselves.[2]

Cicero thinks Casca is exaggerating.

Cicero leaves, and Cassius arrives to meet Casca.

A man no mightier than thyself or me.

'Tis Caesar that you mean.

Cassius says one man is responsible for the anger of the gods. They think Caesar wants to rule alone.

Indeed they say the senators tomorrow mean to establish Caesar as a king.

I know where I will wear this dagger then.

So every bondman[3] in his own hand bears[4] the power to cancel his captivity.

If they don't want to be ruled, Caesar must die.

Cinna the senator arrives. Cassius has already convinced him and other senators to help. They'll be ready to kill Caesar once his friend Brutus is on their side.

Take this paper...lay it in the praetor's[6] chair...

...where Brutus may but find it.

Three parts of him is ours already...

...and the man entire, upon the next encounter, yields him ours.

O Cassius, if you could but win the noble Brutus to our party.[5]

Casca and Cassius will go to Brutus' house to try to persuade him to help them with the plot.

1. strange-disposed: odd.   2. But men . . . themselves: People tend to interpret things in their own way, and may not understand the real meaning at all.   3. bondman: slave.   4. bears: holds.   5. win . . . party: convince Brutus to join us.
6. praetor: senior magistrate – a position in the senate held by Brutus.

BRUTUS, MAN OF THE PEOPLE

Meanwhile...

It must be by his death: and, for my part I know no personal cause to spurn at him...

...but for the general.[1]

Brutus cannot sleep, and paces through his orchard, deep in thought.

Get me a taper[2] in my study, Lucius. When it is lighted, come and call me here.

I found this paper, thus sealed up, and I am sure it did not lie there when I went to bed.

Lucius returns, and shows Brutus a piece of paper he found lying on the floor. It calls him to take action in Rome's name.

Rome is a Republic,[3] and shouldn't be ruled by one man. Brutus knows he has to kill Caesar.

'Brutus, thou sleep'st. Awake and see thyself...

Speak, strike, redress!'[4]

O Rome, I make thee promise, if the redress will follow,...

...thou receivest thy full petition...

...at the hand of Brutus.

The plotters enter the garden, led by Cassius.

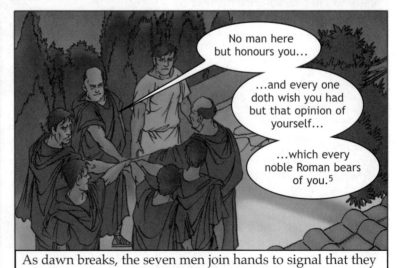

No man here but honours you...

...and every one doth wish you had but that opinion of yourself...

...which every noble Roman bears of you.[5]

As dawn breaks, the seven men join hands to signal that they are all dedicated to the plot.

1. I know . . . general: I have no personal reason to attack him, apart from for the benefit of the Roman people.
2. taper: candle.   3. Republic: a country that is not led by a monarch, but by elected representatives.
4. redress: rectify a wrong.   5. No man...bears of you: Every noble Roman respects you (Caesar), and we all wish you had the same opinion of yourself.

I think it is not meet[1] Mark Antony, so well beloved of Caesar, should outlive Caesar.

Think not of him, for he can do no more than Caesar's arm when Caesar's head is off.

Cassius urges them to kill Mark Antony as well, but Brutus says they should kill only Caesar – otherwise they will seem like criminals.

But it is doubtful yet whether Caesar will come forth today or no.[2]

Never fear that. If he be so resolved,[3] I can o'ersway him.[4]

Make me acquainted with[5] your cause of grief.

I am not well in health, and that is all.

You have some sick offence[6] within your mind, which...I ought to know of.

Brutus' wife Portia wants to know why he has been acting strangely. She begs him to tell the truth.

One of the plotters, Decius, will make sure Caesar comes to the Senate House.

Portia, go in awhile.

And by and by[7] thy bosom shall partake the secrets of my heart.

There is a knock at the door.

The senator Ligarius arrives.

I am not sick, if Brutus have in hand[8] any exploit worthy the name of honour.

Ligarius seems ill, but says he will feel better if Brutus admits to taking part in the conspiracy.

Such an exploit have I in hand...had you a healthful ear to hear of it.

What it is, my Caius,[9] I shall unfold to thee,[10] as we are going to whom it must be done.[11]

Ligarius declares that his sickness has left him at hearing this news. Brutus explains the plot.

1. not meet: not right.　2. no: not.　3. if he be so resolved: if that's what he decides.　4. o'ersway him: change his mind.　5. Make me acquainted with: Let me know.　6. sick offence: horrible deed.　7. by and by: soon.
8. have in hand: is planning.　9. Caius: Ligarius' first name.　10. unfold to thee: reveal to you.　11. to whom it must be done: to the person (Caesar) to whom the deed must be done.

Caesar's Dilemma

Dawn, at Caesar's palace…

Caesar is troubled. His wife Calpurnia slept badly and spoke in her sleep.

He tells his servants to ask the priests what the day will hold for him.

Calpurnia comes to his side, worried that he is in danger.

The beast sacrificed by the priests had no heart. This is a bad omen. Caesar should not go out today, but he is determined.

Calpurnia suggests that Caesar send Mark Antony to the senate in his place.

1. Thrice: Three times.   2. What . . . gods?: How can we avoid anything that the gods have decided?
3. without a heart: without courage.   4. your wisdom is consumed in confidence: your bravery is foolish.

For his wife's sake, Caesar agrees.

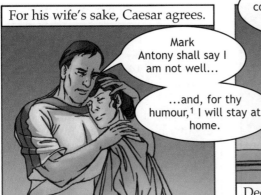

Mark Antony shall say I am not well...

...and, for thy humour,[1] I will stay at home.

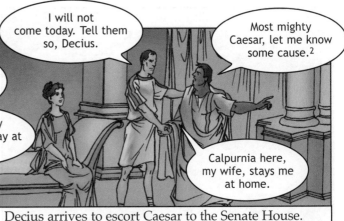

I will not come today. Tell them so, Decius.

Most mighty Caesar, let me know some cause.[2]

Calpurnia here, my wife, stays me at home.

Decius arrives to escort Caesar to the Senate House.

Caesar says Calpurnia dreamed of a statue of him, dripping with blood.

The people dipped their hands into it.

The Senate have concluded to give...

...a crown to mighty Caesar.

Decius thinks the dream is actually a good omen.

How foolish do your fears seem now, Calpurnia! I am ashamed I did yield to them.[3]

Give me my robe, for I will go.

Caesar's ambition gets the better of him.

I have an hour's talk in store for you. Remember that you call on me today. Be near me, that I may remember you.[4]

The conspirators arrive to escort Caesar to the Capitol. He says he has great things planned.

Caesar bids the men to share some wine with him before they leave for the Capitol. Brutus hangs back, pondering the plot.

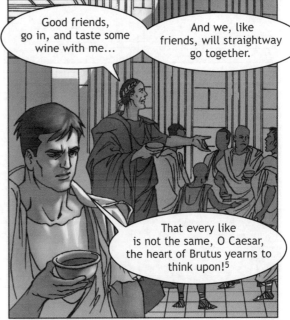

Good friends, go in, and taste some wine with me...

And we, like friends, will straightway go together.

That every like is not the same, O Caesar, the heart of Brutus yearns to think upon![5]

1. for thy humour: so you won't worry.   2. let me know some cause: tell me why.
3. I did yield to them: I let them affect my decision.   4. remember you: praise you to the senate.
5. That every . . . think upon: I am sorry to think that we may not be quite the friends that you believe.

THE LAST CHANCE

But Caesar still has allies...

Caesar, beware of Brutus.
Take heed of Cassius.
Come not near Casca.
Have an eye to Cinna.
Trust not Trebonius.
Mark well Metellus Cimber.
Decius Brutus loves thee not.
Thou hast wronged Caius Ligarius.

Artemidorus has written a letter to Caesar, warning him of the plot.

There is but one mind in all these men, and it is bent against Caesar.

If thou be'st not immortal, look about you: security gives way to conspiracy.

The mighty gods defend thee!

He rushes through Rome to deliver it to Caesar.

Meanwhile...

Bring me word, boy, if thy lord look well, for he went sickly forth.

Brutus' wife Portia is worried about her husband. She sends the slave Lucius to check on him.

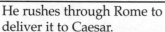

Thou hast some suit[1] to Caesar, hast thou not?

That I have, lady. If it will please Caesar to be so good to Caesar as to hear me...

...I shall beseech him to befriend himself.[2]

The soothsayer rushes around the corner.

Why, know'st thou any harm's intended towards him?

None that I know will be, much that I fear may chance.

The soothsayer sees the crowd approaching and rushes to join it. He cannot give Portia a straight answer.

1. suit: request.   2. beseech him to befriend himself: urge him to look after his own interests.

Portia fears the plot will be discovered.

Caesar makes his way down the narrow streets. Artemidorus chases after the crowd with his letter.

Caesar sees the soothsayer who earlier predicted bad fortune on the Ides of March.

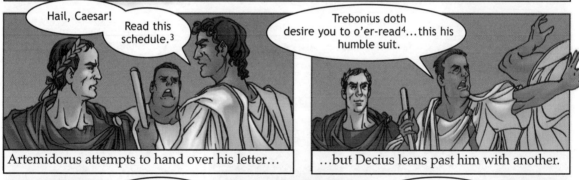

Artemidorus attempts to hand over his letter…

…but Decius leans past him with another.

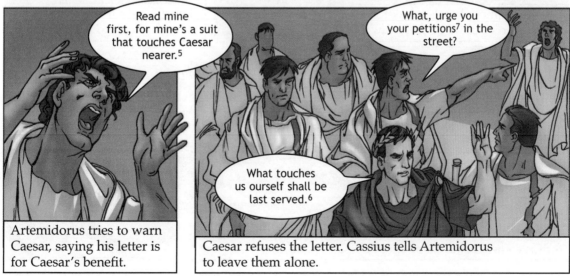

Artemidorus tries to warn Caesar, saying his letter is for Caesar's benefit.

Caesar refuses the letter. Cassius tells Artemidorus to leave them alone.

1. speed: favour.   2. enterprise: plan.   3. schedule: request.   4. o'er-read: read over.   5. touches Caesar nearer: affects Caesar more closely.   6. What touches . . . served: I'll deal with things that affect me last of all. (Caesar means he'll look after the affairs of the people as his first priority.)   7. petitions: requests.

MURDER IN THE SENATE

The senators of Rome make their way to the Senate House.

Trebonius knows his time,[1] for...he draws Mark Antony out of the way.

What is now amiss that Caesar and his Senate must redress?[2]

As the senators gather inside, Cassius and Brutus are nervous. Trebonius leads Mark Antony outside.

Caesar starts the session.

Thy brother by decree[3] is banished.

If thou dost bend, and pray, and fawn[4] for him...

...I spurn[5] thee like a cur[6] out of my way.

Is there no voice more worthy than my own, to sound more sweetly in great Caesar's ear?

Metellus Cimber kneels to ask for his brother's exile to be withdrawn.

Metellus asks if any other person will plead for his brother.

I kiss thy hand, but not in flattery, Caesar.

Desiring thee that[7] Publius Cimber may have an immediate freedom of repeal.[8]

Brutus comes forward and kisses Caesar's hand.

1. knows his time: acts on cue.   2. What is . . . redress?: What wrongs are there that we need to put right?
3. by decree: by the judgement of the courts.   4. fawn: beg.   5. spurn: kick.   6. cur: mongrel.
7. Desiring thee that: I want you to allow.   8. freedom of repeal: pardon.

Caesar cannot disguise his shock. He senses that Brutus is turning against him.

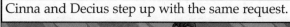

Caesar realises that he is being surrounded.

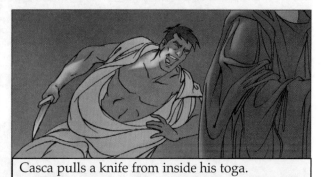

Casca pulls a knife from inside his toga.

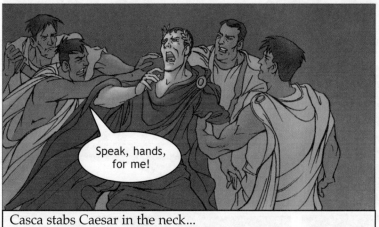

Casca stabs Caesar in the neck...

...and the others join in.

Finally, Brutus stabs his old friend as well.

The deed is done. The senators rejoice.

1. *Et tu, Brute?*: Latin for 'Even you, Brutus?' Caesar cannot believe his friend's betrayal.

95

MARK ANTONY: FRIEND OR FOE?

People and senators, be not affrighted[1]...

Fly not,[2] stand still. Ambition's debt is paid.[3]

Brutus reassures the shocked senators that the worst is over.

There is no harm intended to your person, nor to no Roman else.

So often shall the knot[4] of us be called the men that gave their country liberty.

A terrified old senator wonders if he'll be next. Mark Antony has run away to his house.

Let us bathe our hands in Caesar's blood up to the elbows.

Tell him, so please him come[6] unto this place...

...he shall be satisfied and, by my honour, depart untouched.

Mark Antony shall not love Caesar dead so well as Brutus living.[5]

I know that we shall have him well to friend.[7]

But yet have I a mind that fears him much.[8]

Mark Antony's servant says his master wishes to speak with them.

Brutus is confident, but Cassius is unsure.

96   1. affrighted: afraid.   2. Fly not: Don't run away.   3. Ambition's debt is paid: Caesar has paid the price for his ambition.   4. knot: group.   5. Mark Antony . . . living: Mark Antony will switch his loyalty to Brutus.   6. so please him come: let him come.   7. we shall . . . friend: he'll be a good ally.   8. yet have . . . much: I'm still wary of him.

Mark Antony kneels in horror before the body of his dead friend. If they plan to kill him too, he will die gladly.

Brutus says they mean him no harm.

He asks Mark Antony to wait until everything has been explained to the people.

Mark Antony pretends to go along with the plan, and shakes each of the murderers' hands.

He tells them he will display Caesar's corpse to the outside world, and explain their actions to the people of Rome...

...but secretly he has another plan.

After the others have left, Antony is alone with the body. He praises Caesar and swears revenge.

1. shrunk . . . measure: reduced to this (a dead body).   2. No place . . . by Caesar: I would be happiest to die now, alongside Caesar.   3. leaden points: blunt points, like a practice sword.   4. appeased the multitude: calmed the ordinary citizens.   5. render: offer.   6. as becomes a friend: as a friend should.   7. order: ritual.

SPEECHES TO THE PEOPLE

Meanwhile...

As Brutus and Cassius make their way into the forum,[1] the citizens swarm around them, demanding to know what has happened.

Climbing onto a rostrum,[3] Brutus argues that Caesar was killed for the sake of Rome.

Mark Antony carries Caesar's body towards the rostrum.

Brutus asks if he should kill himself too. The people are won over, and tell him not to.

He asks them all not to flatter him, and to stay to listen to Mark Antony's speech.

Mark Antony plans to turn the crowd against Brutus and the other assassins.

1. forum: a large, open, meeting place.   2. If then that friend demand: If someone asks.   3. rostrum: a raised platform.
4. depart: finish my speech.   5. lover: friend.   6. when it . . . death: when the people of my country want me to die.
7. entreat: ask politely.   8. save I alone: apart from me.

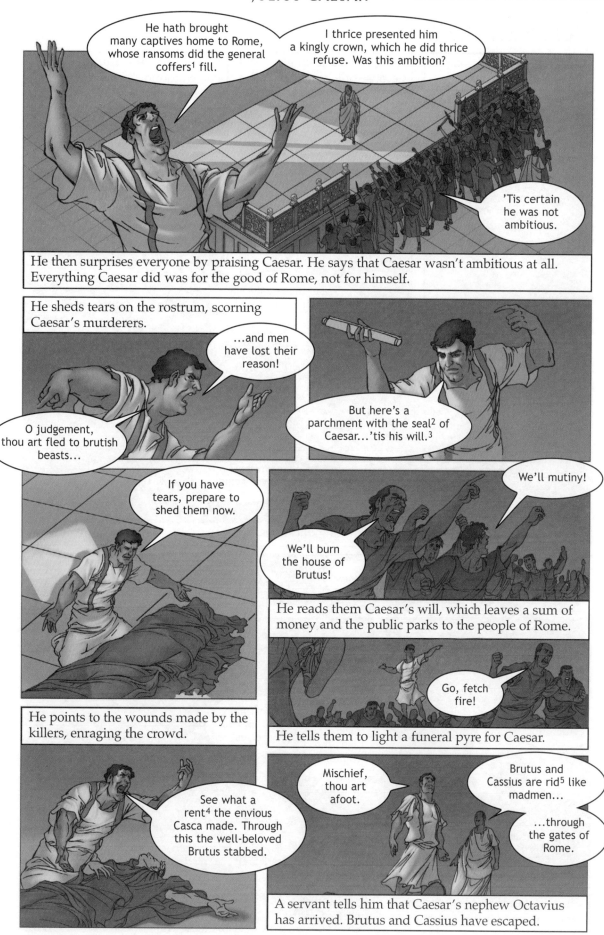

He hath brought many captives home to Rome, whose ransoms did the general coffers[1] fill.

I thrice presented him a kingly crown, which he did thrice refuse. Was this ambition?

'Tis certain he was not ambitious.

He then surprises everyone by praising Caesar. He says that Caesar wasn't ambitious at all. Everything Caesar did was for the good of Rome, not for himself.

He sheds tears on the rostrum, scorning Caesar's murderers.

...and men have lost their reason!

O judgement, thou art fled to brutish beasts...

But here's a parchment with the seal[2] of Caesar...'tis his will.[3]

If you have tears, prepare to shed them now.

We'll mutiny!

We'll burn the house of Brutus!

He reads them Caesar's will, which leaves a sum of money and the public parks to the people of Rome.

Go, fetch fire!

He points to the wounds made by the killers, enraging the crowd.

He tells them to light a funeral pyre for Caesar.

See what a rent[4] the envious Casca made. Through this the well-beloved Brutus stabbed.

Mischief, thou art afoot.

Brutus and Cassius are rid[5] like madmen...

...through the gates of Rome.

A servant tells him that Caesar's nephew Octavius has arrived. Brutus and Cassius have escaped.

1. general coffers: state funds.   2. seal: a mark made in wax, used to show a document was genuine.
3. will: a legal document giving instructions for disposing of a dead person's property.   4. rent: wound
5. are rid: have ridden.

REVENGE

Cinna the poet is walking along a nearby street.

He has a bad feeling because of a dream he had.

I dreamt tonight that I did feast with Caesar...

...and things unluckily charge my fantasy.[1]

Suddenly a crowd of citizens come around the corner carrying torches and makeshift weapons.

What is your name?

Where do you dwell?

Whither[2] are you going?

They surround Cinna, jostling him and asking questions.

Directly, I am going to Caesar's funeral.

I dwell by the Capitol...

Truly, my name is Cinna.

Tear him to pieces! He's a conspirator.

I am not Cinna the conspirator!

Tear him for his bad verses!

They mistake him for the Cinna who conspired against Caesar.

1. Things unluckily charge my fantasy: Events make me worry that I might end up dead too.
2. Whither: Where.

Mad for blood, the mob kills Cinna.

Mark Antony, Octavius and Lepidus meet to look over the names of Caesar's murderers, which include Lepidus' brother...

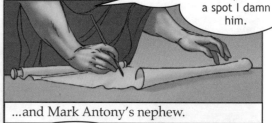

...and Mark Antony's nephew.

Lepidus is sent to fetch Caesar's real will.

Mark Antony doesn't think Lepidus deserves a part in their triumvirate[5]...

...but he will be good for simple tasks for as long as he is needed.

Octavius and Mark Antony plan to gather allies for an attack on Brutus and Cassius.

1. Consent you?: Do you agree?   2. We shall . . . legacies: We'll work out a plan to save some of the money that was promised to the people.   3. unmeritable: unworthy.   4. meet to be sent on errands: fit to be sent to perform minor tasks.
5. triumvirate: a leadership team of three people.   6. Then take we . . . empty ass: Then we send him away like a useless donkey.   7. our means stretched: our power combined.

Uneasy Allies

Several months later...

Brutus has amassed his forces in Sardis,[1] ready to face the armies of Octavius and Mark Antony. Since leaving Rome, Brutus and Cassius have grown cautious of each other.

I do not doubt but that my noble master will appear such as he is, full of regard and honour.[2]

A soldier brings the news that Cassius will soon arrive.

Thou hast described a hot friend cooling.

Cassius and his army arrive.

Stand, ho! Speak the word along.[3]

Stand.

Stand.

Let us not wrangle.[4]

Bid them move away.[5]

Brutus refuses to argue before his troops.

You yourself are much condemned to have an itching palm.[6]

You know that you are Brutus that speak this, or, by the gods, this speech were else your last.[7]

Cassius is angry with Brutus for prosecuting his friend, the governor of Sardis, for taking bribes. Brutus points out that Cassius himself is known to take bribes.

1. Sardis: a city now known as Sart, located in the west of Turkey.   2. I do not doubt . . . honour: I have no doubt that Cassius will be here soon, eager to join you again.   3. Speak the word along: Pass the order to stand along the line. 4. wrangle: argue.   5. Bid them move away: Ask the soldiers to go away.   6. condemned . . . palm: accused of being greedy.   7. You know . . . else your last: If you weren't Brutus, I'd kill you for saying this.

The pair exchange insults. Brutus believes that they killed Caesar to make Rome better, and that Cassius' dishonesty makes a mockery of this aim.

Away, slight man!

Urge me no more,[1] I shall forget myself.

You love me not.

I do not like your faults.

Come, Antony and young Octavius, come.

Revenge yourselves alone on Cassius.[2]

Ashamed by his brother-in-law's criticism, Cassius pulls out his dagger to kill himself.

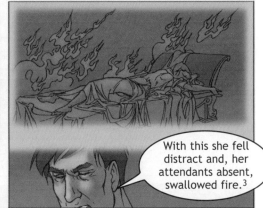

Sheathe your dagger.

Give me your hand.

And my heart too.

Brutus grabs Cassius' hand to stop him harming himself. The argument is over.

Portia is dead.

Brutus is upset because his wife, Portia, became grief-stricken in his absence. She sent her servants away and killed herself in a house fire.

With this she fell distract and, her attendants absent, swallowed fire.[3]

Now sit we close about this taper here.

A messenger, Messala, arrives from Rome.

Messala says that Octavius and Mark Antony have put to death a hundred senators, including Cicero.

1. Urge me no more: Stop provoking me.   2. Revenge yourselves alone on Cassius: Cassius wants to take the punishment for murdering Caesar by taking his own life.   3. swallowed fire: suffocated on the smoke from the fire.

THE GHOST OF CAESAR

Messala tells the generals that Octavius and Mark Antony have marched to nearby Philippi.[1]

The battlefield is sparse and desolate.

'Tis better that the enemy seek us, so shall he waste his means,[2] weary his soldiers.

Cassius wants to wait for their enemy to come to them.

The people 'twixt[3] Philippi and this ground do stand but in a forced affection.[4]

Then, with your will,[5] go on. We'll along[6] ourselves, and meet them at Philippi.

Canst thou hold up thy heavy eyes awhile, and touch thy instrument a strain or two?[7]

However, Brutus believes it is best to head to Philippi first. Cassius concedes to his brother-in-law, and says goodnight.

Brutus calls for his trusted soldiers to keep him company.

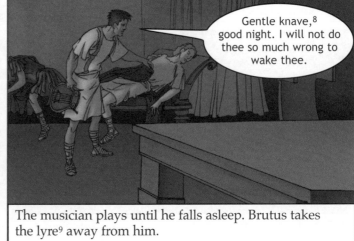

Gentle knave,[8] good night. I will not do thee so much wrong to wake thee.

The music calms Brutus' thoughts.

The musician plays until he falls asleep. Brutus takes the lyre[9] away from him.

1. Philippi: a place in present-day northern Greece. 2. waste his means: use up his supplies. 3. 'twixt: between.
4. do stand . . . affection: are allies only because they fear us (Brutus is worried they will go over to Mark Antony's side).
5. with your wish: as you wish. 6. along: march. 7. touch thy . . . two: play a little music on your instrument.
8. knave: young man. 9. lyre: a stringed musical instrument.

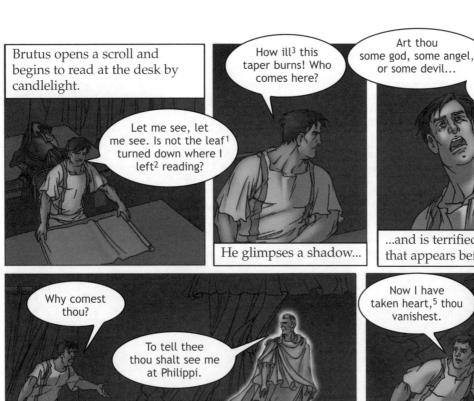

Brutus opens a scroll and begins to read at the desk by candlelight.

Let me see, let me see. Is not the leaf[1] turned down where I left[2] reading?

How ill[3] this taper burns! Who comes here?

He glimpses a shadow...

Art thou some god, some angel, or some devil...

...that makest my blood cold and my hair to stare?[4]

...and is terrified by the shape that appears before him.

Why comest thou?

To tell thee thou shalt see me at Philippi.

The ghost of Caesar stands in the tent doorway.

Now I have taken heart,[5] thou vanishest.

The ghost vanishes, leaving the tent door flapping in the wind.

Boy! Lucius! Varro! Claudius!

Sirs, awake!

Brutus quickly wakes the others.

Didst thou see any thing?

Nor I, my lord.

No, my lord, I saw nothing.

Nothing, my lord.

Go and commend me[6] to my brother Cassius.

Bid him set on his powers betimes before[7] and we will follow.

Brutus orders the soldiers to go to Cassius and stir his troops. It's time to march.

1. leaf: page. (Shakespeare forgets that Roman books were scrolls, and did not have pages.)   2. left: stopped.
3. ill: badly.   4. stare: stand on end.   5. taken heart: recovered my courage.
6. commend me: pass on my greetings.   7. Bid him . . . before: Ask him to ready his troops as soon as possible.

PREPARING FOR BATTLE

On the plains at Philippi the two armies ready themselves for battle: on one side, Octavius and Mark Antony...

...on the other, Brutus and Cassius.

Mark Antony and Octavius discuss tactics.

The leaders ride out onto the battlefield.

Octavius runs out of patience.

1. lead your battle softly on: advance your army with caution.   2. In your...'Hail Caesar!': Mark Antony is saying that Brutus is dishonest, because he praised Caesar ('good words'), after murdering him ('bad strokes').
3. goes up: will be put back in its sheath.   4. three and thirty: Caesar was stabbed thirty-three times.
5. till another . . . traitors: Until he (Octavius Caesar) has been killed as well.

Octavius makes his way back to his army.

Cassius speaks to the messenger Messala.

He tells of an omen he witnessed.

Brutus comes back to Cassius' side.

Brutus says that even though suicide is the traditional custom in defeat, it is cowardly.
Cassius asks if he will let himself be captured in that case. Brutus says he will not.

1. Unless . . . thee: Unless there are traitors in your own army.   2. peevish: silly, moody.   3. when you have
stomachs: when you are brave enough.   4. in their steads: in place of them.   5. ravens, crows and kites: birds that
are bad omens before a battle, because they are scavengers that feed on dead bodies.   6. bound: chained like a prisoner.
7. bears too great a mind: is too noble-minded to submit to imprisonment.

The Chaos of Battle

On the plains of Philippi, the two sides meet in battle…

Let them set on[1] at once. For I perceive but cold demeanour[2] in Octavius' wing, and sudden push gives them the overthrow.[3]

Ride, ride, Messala. let them all come down.

Brutus gives Messala orders to tell what's left of his troops to attack Octavius' forces.

Meanwhile, Cassius' troops have fled.

The villains fly![4] Myself have to mine own turned enemy.[5]

This ensign[6] here of mine was turning back…

I slew[7] the coward, and did take it from him.

Cassius saw his own standard-bearer fleeing, and killed him.

1. set on: attack. 2. cold demeanour: lack of spirit for the fight. 3. gives them the overthrow: will overthrow them. 4. fly: run away. 5. Myself have . . . enemy: My men are deserting me. 6. ensign: standard-bearer. He carried the eagle emblem which Roman soldiers followed into battle 7. slew: killed.

Titinius, an officer in Cassius' army, says that Brutus sent his men in too early. Now they are looting instead of fighting.

Brutus...who, having some advantage on Octavius, took it too eagerly.

His soldiers fell to spoil,[1] whilst we by Antony are all enclosed.[2]

Fly further off, my lord... Mark Antony is in your tents, my lord.

Mark Antony's troops are destroying Cassius' camp, setting fire to the tents and killing the servants.

Cassius' slave, Pindarus, urges him to retreat.

Soon Pindarus reports that Titinius has been captured. He was seen surrounded by soldiers. Cassius is overwhelmed with grief.

Now be a freeman, and with this good sword, that ran through Caesar's bowels, search this bosom.[3]

Cassius hands his sword to Pindarus. He will give him his freedom if he'll carry out one final task – to kill his master.

O, coward that I am, to live so long to see my best friend taken before my face!

Far from this country Pindarus shall run, where never Roman shall take note of[4] him.

Pindarus obeys. He kills Cassius and rides off.

1. having some . . . fell to spoil: while the soldiers had the upper hand, they started looting.   2. enclosed: surrounded.
3. search this bosom: stab me in the chest.   4. take note of: notice.

THE SHAME OF DEFEAT

But Titinius isn't dead...

It is but change, Titinius...

...for Octavius is overthrown by noble Brutus' power, as Cassius' legions are by Antony.

Pindarus thought he saw him captured by the enemy, but he was actually riding with allies.

Titinius approaches with Messala, who says that the outcome is uncertain.

These tidings would well comfort Cassius.[1]

He lies not like the living.

O my heart!

He catches sight of Cassius' body on the ground.

Messala goes to find Brutus. Meanwhile, overcome with grief, Titinius takes Cassius' sword...

By your leave, gods: this is a Roman's part[2]...

O setting sun, as in thy red rays thou dost sink to night...

...so in his red blood Cassius' day is set, the sun of Rome is set! Where art thou, Pindarus!

...and kills himself as well.

Come, Cassius' sword, and find Titinius' heart.

1. These tidings . . . Cassius: Although Cassius' forces are losing, he'll be glad that Brutus' are doing better.
2. this is a Roman's part: this (suicide) is a fitting way for a Roman to behave.

Where, where, Messala, doth his body lie?

Lo, yonder, and Titinius mourning it.

A crowd of other soldiers arrive, including Messala and Brutus.

Seeing that Titinius is dead, Brutus remembers Caesar's ghost appearing to him.

Titinius' face is upward.

O Julius Caesar, thou art mighty yet!¹

Thy spirit walks abroad,² and turns our swords in our own proper entrails.³

He can see that the battle is almost lost…

…but he rouses his men for one final fight.

Lucilius, come. And come, young Cato. Let us to the field.

Labeo and Flavius, set our battles on.

'Tis three o'clock, and, Romans, yet ere night⁴ we shall try fortune⁵ in a second fight.

The remaining forces rush into battle.

1. yet: still.   2. abroad: away from its proper place, in the underworld.   3. in our own proper entrails: into our own stomachs.   4. yet ere night: before nightfall.   5. try fortune: try our luck.

The Final Throw of the Dice

Brutus leads his men forward.

He and Cato see Mark Antony's forces waiting.

Cato and Lucilius ride to the enemy.

Cato throws himself into the shield wall...

...and meets his death.

Enemy soldiers surround Lucilius. Pretending to be Brutus, he offers the soldiers money to kill him.

1. art thou down?: are you dead?   2. There is . . . straight: Here's enough money to pay you to kill me immediately.

But the soldiers don't want to kill such an important prisoner.

Mark Antony asks to see Brutus.

Lucilius reveals his true identity, and declares that Brutus would never allow himself to be captured.

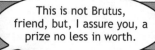

Mark Antony is not angry that it isn't Brutus. He admires Lucilius' sacrifice.

Mark Antony returns to his tent, and gives orders to find the real Brutus.

1. ta'en: taken, captured.   2. how everything is chanced: what has happened.

The Death of a Noble Roman

At the edge of the battlefield, Brutus regroups his remaining men.

Come, poor remains of friends, rest on this rock.

Brutus whispers something into Clitus' ear.

What, I, my lord? No, not for all the world.

Shall I do such a deed?

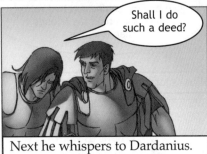

Next he whispers to Dardanius.

Clitus asks Dardanius what Brutus wanted.

The ghost of Caesar hath appeared to me two several[3] times by night...

...at Sardis once, and this last night here in Philippi fields.

I know my hour is come.

Not so, my lord.

Brutus now addresses Volumnius.

What ill[1] request did Brutus make to thee?

To kill him, Clitus. Look, he meditates.[2]

I prithee,[4] hold thou my sword-hilts, whilst I run on it.

1. ill: awful, terrible.   2. meditates: thinks deeply.   3, several: separate.   4. I prithee: I beg you.

Clitus warns that the enemy is closing in. Brutus says he'll escape with them...

...but he does not intend to run.

Brutus looks to the heavens.

He pulls himself onto the sword, and dies.

Octavius appears, with Messala and Lucilius as his captives.

The battle is won. Mark Antony pays tribute to Brutus. Even though he killed Caesar, he alone did so with honourable motives.

Messala asks Strato what has happened to Brutus.

1. tarrying: delaying.   2. respect: reputation.   3. I killed . . . a will: I found it harder to kill you than I find it to kill myself.   4. bondage: the prison of life.
5. can but . . . fire of him: can only place him on a funeral pyre.   6. All the . . . Caesar: All the other conspirators, apart from Brutus, killed Caesar through envy.

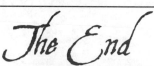

Romeo & Juliet

William Shakespeare

Illustrated by

Penko Gelev

Retold by

Jim Pipe

Series created and designed by

David Salariya

O Romeo, Romeo, wherefore art thou Romeo? Deny thy father and refuse thy name, or if thou wilt not, be but sworn my love, and I'll no longer be a Capulet. (*see page 133*).

CHARACTERS

Romeo

Juliet

Mercutio,
Romeo's friend

Tybalt, Juliet's cousin

Friar Laurence

Nurse

Lord Capulet, Juliet's father

Lady Capulet, Juliet's
mother

Lord Montague,
Romeo's father

Lady Montague,
Romeo's mother

Paris

Benvolio,
Romeo's cousin

Escalus, Prince of
Verona

TWO FAMILIES AT WAR

In Verona, a town in north Italy, two noble families, the Montagues and the Capulets, are at war because of an 'ancient grudge'.

From these houses, two 'star-crossed'[1] young lovers will mend the quarrel between their families by falling in love – and dying. Read on to find out how their tragic story unfolds...

All seems quiet in Verona's busy piazza.[2]

Draw thy tool! Here comes of the house of Montagues.

My naked weapon is out: quarrel,[3] I will back thee.

However, two Capulets, Sampson and Gregory, are hungry for a fight.

Do you bite your thumb[4] at us, sir?

No, sir, I do not bite my thumb at you, sir, but I bite my thumb, sir.

They run into Abraham and Balthasar, two Montagues. Sampson tries to provoke Abraham by making a rude gesture.

Do you quarrel, sir?

Quarrel sir? No, sir.

The men know they should not argue in a public place, but Abraham quickly rises to the bait.

I serve as good a man as you.

No better.

Sampson claims the Capulets are better than the Montagues.

Yes, better, sir.

You lie.

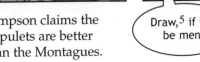

Draw,[5] if you be men.

A fight breaks out...

1. star-crossed: ill-fated.   2. piazza: public square.
3. quarrel: start an argument.
4. bite your thumb: a rude gesture, done by flicking your thumb out from behind your front teeth.
5. draw: pull out your sword.

THE PRINCE'S WARNING

Benvolio,[1] a Montague, arrives and tries to separate the angry men.

Just then, Tybalt, Lord Capulet's hot-headed nephew, joins the men. Spoiling for a fight, he draws his sword on Benvolio.

Benvolio tries to calm things down. But Tybalt causes trouble.

Tybalt attacks Benvolio.

Before anyone is injured, a group of local citizens intervene, armed with weapons. They try to break up the fight.

Hearing the noise, Lord Capulet rushes to join in. Lady Capulet mocks her aged husband.

On the opposite side of the piazza, Lady Montague also tries to restrain her husband.

---

1. Benvolio's name means 'well-wisher'.   2. drawn: with your sword in your hand.
122   3. bills and partisans: two types of pike – hooked spears at the end of a long pole.   4. crutch: walking aid.

Rebellious subjects, enemies to peace!

Throw your mistempered[1] weapons to the ground.

Three civil brawls,[2] bred of an airy[3] word...

... have thrice[4] disturbed the quiet of our streets.

Suddenly, Prince Escalus, the ruler of Verona, steps in to halt the violence. He is tired of the disruptions caused by the two feuding families.

Seeing the Prince and his soldiers, the Montagues and Capulets stop fighting. The Prince is furious: it's the third time they've fought on the streets of Verona.

If ever you disturb our streets again, your lives shall pay the forfeit[5] of the peace.

O, where is Romeo? Saw you him today?

Later...

Underneath the grove of sycamore... So early walking did I see your son.

The Prince issues a stern warning: any Capulets and Montagues caught fighting will be executed.

Reluctantly, the Capulets and Montagues leave the piazza, but the tension between the two families remains.

Lord and Lady Montague ask Benvolio if he has seen their son Romeo. Romeo has been acting strangely recently.

Many a morning he has been there seen...

My noble uncle, do you know the cause?

Could we but learn from whence[7] his sorrows grow, we would as willingly give cure as know.

I neither know it nor can learn of him.

...with tears augmenting[6] the fresh morning's dew.

Lord Montague has tried to find out why Romeo is so depressed, but his son keeps his feelings to himself.

1. mistempered: wrongly made or 'tempered', because they are being used by people in a bad temper.   2. brawls: fights.
3. airy: vague – no-one knows exactly why the Montagues and Capulets are fighting.   4. thrice: three times.
5. forfeit: penalty for breaking the peace.   6. augmenting: adding to.   7. whence: from what cause.

LOVESTRUCK ROMEO

Benvolio runs into Romeo in a sidestreet. Benvolio asks why his friend is looking so upset.

Romeo confides that he is in love with a girl, Rosaline, who does not return his affections.

Benvolio advises Romeo to forget Rosaline and find another woman.

Romeo isn't convinced – he believes he will never forget Rosaline's beauty.

1. morrow: morning.   2. Not having… short: Not having the thing that makes time pass quickly.
3. in sadness: seriously.   4. Be ruled be me: Take my advice.   5. By giving liberty to your eyes: Allow your eyes to wander.   6. Thou canst not: You can't.

Meanwhile...

'Tis not hard, I think, for men so old as we to keep the peace.

Paris, a relative of the Prince of Verona, is talking to Lord Capulet. Paris hopes to marry Lord Capulet's daughter, Juliet.

Lord Capulet knows both he and Lord Montague are troubled by the latest fight between their young relatives.

But now, my lord, what say you to my suit?[1]

My child is yet a stranger in the world. She hath not seen the change of fourteen years.[2]

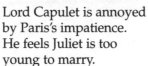

Younger than she are happy mothers made.

Paris nods in agreement, but he's keen to talk about his marriage to Juliet.

Lord Capulet is annoyed by Paris's impatience. He feels Juliet is too young to marry.

Capulet wants Paris to wait two more years, but Paris protests – girls younger than Juliet are mothers.[3]

But woo her, gentle Paris, get her heart.

This night I hold an old accustomed feast.

Come, go with me.

Lord Capulet reminds Paris he has to win Juliet over before he will agree to their marriage.

Capulet invites Paris to a masquerade[4] he is holding that night, in the hope that Paris will capture Juliet's heart.

---

1. suit: marriage proposal.   2. She hath… fourteen years: She isn't even 14 yet.
3. mothers: in those times, 13-year-old girls were often married with children.
4. masquerade: a ball where the guests wear masks.

AN INVITATION TO THE FEAST

Find those persons out whose names are written there.

God gi'-good-e'en.[2] I pray sir, can you read?

Ay, mine own fortune in my misery.[3]

Later that day, Lord Capulet gives his servant a list of people to invite to the masquerade.

Unfortunately, the servant can't read.[1] He heads off in search of someone who can.

Romeo and Benvolio, who are still discussing Romeo's broken heart, bump into the servant. He asks them for help.

My master is the great rich Capulet, and if you be not of the house of Montagues, I pray come and crush a cup of wine.[5]

Compare her face with some that I shall show...

Whither[4] should they come?

...And I will make thee think thy swan a crow.

Romeo reads the letter. He's impressed by the guest list – Rosaline is invited! He wonders who is throwing such a party.

The servant leaves. Benvolio tells Romeo to sneak into the feast, to see if his Rosaline matches up to the other beauties attending.

One fairer than my love? The all-seeing sun ne'er[6] saw her match since first the world begun.

Nurse... Hear our counsel.[7]

Romeo doesn't believe there is anyone in the world prettier than Rosaline.

Meanwhile, in the Capulets' mansion, young Juliet talks to her mother, Lady Capulet, and her Nurse.[8]

1. can't read: in the 16th century only nobles and certain tradesmen were taught to read.
2. God gi'-good-e'en: God give you good evening.   3. Ay... misery: Romeo is making a grim joke about 'reading', or realising, the sadness in his own life.   4. whither: to what place.   5. come... of wine: come for a drink.
6. ne'er: never.   7: counsel: discussion.   8. Nurse: the woman who helped bring Juliet up as a baby.

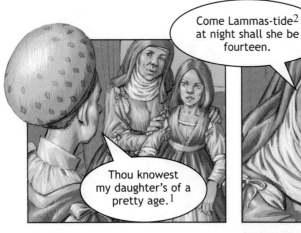

Come Lammas-tide[2] at night shall she be fourteen.

Thou knowest my daughter's of a pretty age.[1]

Thou wast the prettiest babe that e'er I nursed.

The three of them discuss Juliet's marriage to Paris. Lady Capulet asks the Nurse to persuade Juliet that Paris is a fine match.

The Nurse proudly says she knows exactly how old Juliet is – she isn't fourteen yet.

The Nurse hugs Juliet affectionately as she remembers breast-feeding her as a baby.[3]

How stands your disposition to be married?[4]

Well, think of marriage now... The valiant[5] Paris seeks you for his love.

It is an honour that I dream not of.

He's a flower, in faith a very flower.[6]

Hearing enough, Lady Capulet impatiently asks the Nurse to be quiet and gets to the heart of the matter: Does Juliet want to marry?

Can you like of Paris' love?

I'll look to like, if looking liking move.

Lady Capulet is determined to get an answer from Juliet. The marriage is important to the family as Paris is related to the Prince of Verona, but she also wants Juliet to be happy.

Juliet hardly knows her future husband, but she agrees to take a good look at Paris during the feast to see if she could grow to love him.

1. Thou knowest… age: You know she's a good age to marry.   2. Lammas-tide: 1 August, the harvest festival.
3. breast-feeding: it was once common for noble women to have servants, called wet nurses, to feed their babies.
4. How stands… married: How do you feel about getting married?
5. valiant: brave, noble.   6. He's a flower… flower: He's good-looking – very good-looking!

LOVE AT FIRST SIGHT

Evening comes and the Capulet masquerade begins.

I am not for this ambling.[1]

Nay, gentle Romeo, we must have you dance.

Outside in the street, an unhappy Romeo follows Benvolio and their friend Mercutio to Lord Capulet's house.

Come, knock and enter; and no sooner in but every man betake him to his legs.[2]

They put on their masks, but Romeo isn't sure if he wants to go. Benvolio tries to encourage him to have some fun.

I'll be a candle-holder and look on; The game was ne'er so fair, and I am done.[3]

As they reach the Capulet mansion, Romeo offers to hold the torch and watch while the others enjoy themselves.

Tut! Dun's the mouse,[4] the constable's own word![5]

Mercutio warns the others to fade into the crowd – Montagues are not welcome here.

I dreamt a dream tonight.

And so did I.

Romeo is worried – he had a dream that something bad will happen if they enter.

Well, what was yours?

That dreamers often lie.

Mercutio laughs at Romeo, saying he shouldn't worry about dreams – they don't mean anything.

Supper is done, and we shall come too late.

Worried that they will miss the party, Benvolio pushes the others through the door to the Capulet mansion.

1. ambling: dancing.   2. every man... legs: let's all get on the dancefloor.   3. The game... done: I'm going to give up while the going is good.   4. Dun's the mouse: Mercutio is playing with Romeo's last word – 'done'. 'Dun' means dark and brown, like a mouse, so he's comparing Romeo to a quiet mouse.   5. the constable's own word: a policeman always tells his men to be quiet when catching a criminal – don't get caught at the party!

They walk towards the busy banquet hall. Servants are running this way and that, shouting at each other.

As the three friends enter the Great Chamber, they see Lord Capulet welcoming his guests.

Capulet likes to see his guests dancing, but he feels too old to join in!

Meanwhile, Romeo sees Juliet from across the room, as she takes her mask off. He falls in love on the spot, without even knowing Juliet's name.

In a trance, Romeo has already forgotten his former love, Rosaline.

However, Tybalt, Lord Capulet's nephew, recognises Romeo. Furious, he orders his servant to bring him his sword.

Lord Capulet wonders what is going on. Tybalt tells him he has seen Romeo, and is determined to start a fight.

Though Capulet holds him back, Tybalt swears to take revenge for their intrusion.

1. Great Chamber: main dining room.   2. she hangs… ear: she lights up the night like a sparkling jewel hanging next to black African skin.   3. Forswear it: Deny it.   4. rapier: a long, thin sword.   5. Wherefore storm you so?: Why are you so angry?   6. foe: enemy.   7. This intrusion… gall: Crashing the party may seem like fun now, but the Montagues will bitterly regret it.

The Lovers Meet

My lips, two blushing pilgrims,[1] ready stand to smooth that rough touch with a tender kiss.

Unaware of the threat from Tybalt, Romeo boldly takes Juliet's hand and leads her to a quiet spot away from the other guests. He apologises for his roughness.

Juliet too has fallen in love…

Good pilgrim, you do wrong your hand too much… palm to palm is holy palmer's[2] kiss.[3]

Let lips do what hands do!

Lost in each other, the two young lovers kiss, then kiss again.

You kiss by th' book.[4]

Madam, your mother craves a word[5] with you.

What is her mother?

Just then, the Nurse interrupts them with a message from Juliet's mother, Lady Capulet.

Reluctantly, Juliet tears herself away, leaving Romeo alone with the Nurse.

Romeo asks the Nurse who Juliet is. Her answer shocks him.

1. pilgrim: a visitor to a holy place – Romeo compares his lips to pilgrims as he worships Juliet's beauty. Romeo's name means 'Pilgrim to Rome' in Italian.   2. palmer: pilgrims carried a palm leaf to show they had been to Jerusalem.   3. palm to… kiss: pilgrims touch hand to hand when they pray.   4. You kiss… book: You kiss like someone who has studied romantic novels – in other words, very well!   5. craves a word: wants to talk.

Her mother is the lady of the house.

Is she a Capulet? O dear account! My life is my foe's debt.[1]

Away, be gone, the sport is at the best.[2]

Ay, so I fear; the more is my unrest.[3]

Romeo is devastated. He realises he's fallen head over heels in love with a Capulet, his family's bitter enemy.

Hearing the sound of footsteps, Romeo looks up. It's Benvolio. Now Romeo knows who Juliet is, he's happy to leave the party.

I thank you, honest gentlemen. Good night.

Come on, let's to bed.

Seeing them leave, Lord Capulet bids them goodbye.

Benvolio, Romeo and Mercutio leave the Capulet mansion.

Inside, Lord Capulet realises how late it is and heads upstairs with Lady Capulet.

What's he that follows there, that would not dance?

His name is Romeo, and a Montague, the only son of your great enemy.

My only love, sprung from my only hate!

Too early seen unknown, and known too late.[4]

Juliet is keen to know who her handsome stranger is. Her Nurse tells her he is a Montague. Juliet realises she has fallen for someone that she is supposed to hate.

1. Oh dear... debt: There's a terrible price to pay, as I'm dependent on my enemy.
2. the sport... best: the best part of the party is over.
3. the more... unrest: if only you knew why I'm so worried.
4: Too early... late: I saw him too soon as a stranger, and I found out too late who he was.

THE BALCONY

Romeo has fallen in love again – but unlike Rosaline, Juliet loves him in return. Yet, what future can there be for the young lovers when their families are at war?

But Romeo can't get Juliet out of this head. He has to see her again… whatever the risk.

It's still dark when the three friends leave the feast. Romeo drops behind and leaps over the wall into the Capulet orchard.

Romeo! Humours! Madman! Passion! Lover!

I conjure[1] thee by Rosaline's bright eyes.

Benvolio and Mercutio peer over the wall to see where Romeo has gone. Mercutio teases him, hoping Romeo will reveal his hiding place.

Blind is his love and best befits[2] the dark.

When Romeo doesn't appear, Benvolio persuades Mercutio to leave him alone. Mercutio agrees and they merrily head for home.

'Tis in vain, to seek him here that means not to be found.[3]

He jests at scars that never felt a wound.[4]

Romeo hears every word from inside the Capulet orchard. To him, Mercutio's mocking words show he has never been in love.

But soft, what light through yonder window[5] breaks? It is the east, and Juliet is the sun![6]

Creeping nearer the Capulet mansion, Romeo spies Juliet in a window above.

See, how she leans her cheek upon her hand!

O that I were a glove upon that hand, that I might touch that cheek!

As he watches, Juliet comes out onto her balcony and speaks out loud,[7] not realising that Romeo can hear from below.

---

1. conjure: to call up a spirit by saying magic words.   2. befits: suits.   3. 'Tis in... found: It's useless to seek someone who doesn't want to be found.   4. He jests… wound: He laughs because he has never felt the pain of being in love.   5. yonder window: that window (over there).   6. But soft… sun: Romeo imagines Juliet is the sun, rising in the east and spreading its soft light.   7. speaks out loud: in plays, a speech made when someone is alone is called a soliloquy.

Juliet wishes Romeo could give up his family name. If he can't, she will happily change hers so they can be together.

Romeo calls out from the shadows.

Juliet is surprised by the voice, but she guesses who it is in the dark.

Juliet warns Romeo about the danger, but Romeo is confident the darkness will keep him safe.

Juliet must say goodbye, but Romeo climbs the balcony.

Romeo asks Juliet to marry him – she says yes! But for now Romeo must leave. They arrange to meet the next day.

It is almost dawn. Juliet can't bear to say goodbye – it feels like twenty years until tomorrow.

1. wherefore: why – why of all people is Romeo a Montague?   2. That which... sweet: A name means nothing – a rose still smells sweet whatever it is called – Romeo is still Romeo whatever his name is.   3. Call me... baptised: Say you love me and I will take a new name.   4. henceforth: from now on.   5. Art thou not: Aren't you.   6. Dost thou: Do you.
7. thou wilt... word: you'll say yes and I'll believe you.   8. I gave... request it: I have already given you my love.
9. Parting is...sorrow: I'm sad to say goodbye but happy that it's you I'm talking to.

133

A VISIT TO THE FRIAR

Romeo hurries to see his friend Friar Laurence, an expert in making poisons and medicines from plants.

This being tasted, slays all senses with the heart.[1]

Good morrow, father.

Benedicite![2] Where hast thou been?

The Friar is surprised to see Romeo up so early and wonders what he has been up to. He suspects that Romeo must be worrying about something – or he'd still be in bed!

I have been feasting with mine enemy.

My heart's dear love is set on the fair daughter of rich Capulet.

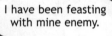

This I pray, that thou consent[3] to marry us today.

Romeo tells the Friar all about meeting Juliet the night before. He begs the Friar to marry them straight away!

Is Rosaline, that thou did love so dear, so soon forsaken?[4]

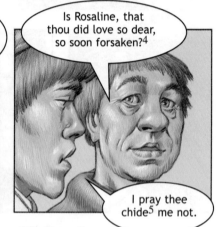

I pray thee chide[5] me not.

The Friar is shocked that Romeo has forgotten Rosaline so quickly.

I'll thy assistant be, for this alliance may so happy prove to turn your households' rancour to pure love.[6]

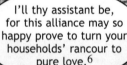

The Friar agrees to help, if only because he hopes their marriage will end the feud between the two families.

O let us hence![7]

Wisely and slow. They stumble that run fast.

Romeo is in a terrible rush, but the Friar warns him to take things slowly to avoid trouble.

1. This being… heart: When swallowed, this flower stops your heart – dead.
2. Benedicite: bless you!   3 consent: agree.   4. forsaken: forgotten, given up.   5: chide: scold, tell off.
134   6. this alliance… love: this marriage may be so fortunate that it will turn the hatred between the two families to love.
7. let us hence: let's get going.

Alas, poor Romeo, he is already dead.

Later that morning...

Mercutio and Benvolio wonder where Romeo is. Tybalt has challenged their friend to a duel.

Mercutio explains...

Why, what is Tybalt?

More than Prince of Cats,[1] I can tell you.

The very butcher of the silk button,[2] a duellist, a duellist!

What counterfeit[3] did I give you?

The slip, sir, the slip![4]

Not long after, Romeo turns up. Mercutio and Benvolio tease him for getting away from them the night before.

Farewell, ancient lady, farewell!

The three are still chatting when the Nurse arrives to meet Romeo, as planned. When Mercutio leaves with Benvolio, he makes fun of the Nurse.

I am so vexed[5] that every part about me quivers. Scurvy knave![6]

The Nurse is furious at Mercutio's cheeky remark. Romeo leads her to a quiet corner of the piazza to explain his plan.

Bid her devise some means to come to shrift[7] this afternoon.

And there she shall at Friar Laurence' cell be shrived[8] and married.

Romeo's servant will bring a rope ladder for the Nurse to smuggle into the Capulet mansion, so he can reach Juliet's room that night.

Commend[9] me to thy lady.

Ay, a thousand times.

The Nurse leaves to tell Juliet of the plan. Romeo calls after her.

---

1. Prince of Cats: Tybalt was the name of the cat in the medieval tale of Reynard the Fox.
2. butcher of the silk button: he slices through clothes like a butcher through meat!   3: counterfeit: fake, fraud.
4: The slip: a fake coin – Mercutio is playing with words when he says Romeo has given them the slip (run away from them).   5. vexed: angry.   6. Scurvy knave: Bold rascal.   7. Bid her...shrift: Tell her to find an excuse to make a confession (with the Friar).   8. shrived: forgiven for her sins.   9. Commend: Remember me kindly, recommend me.

THE MARRIAGE

Back in the Capulet mansion, Juliet waits for news of Romeo.

O honey nurse, what news? Hast thou[1] met with him?

What haste! Do you not see that I am out of breath?

When the Nurse enters, Juliet jumps up excitedly to talk to her.

What says he of our marriage?

Lord, how my head aches!

The Nurse teases Juliet by delaying her answer, but Juliet is impatient to know the plan.

Come, what says Romeo?

Have you got leave to go to shrift[2] today?

At last, the Nurse tells all.

I have.

Then hie[3] you hence[4] to Friar Laurence' cell: there stays a husband to make you a wife.

Hie to high fortune! Honest Nurse, farewell.

Juliet sets off for Friar Laurence's cell straight away.

So smile the heavens upon this holy act, that after-hours with sorrow chide us not![5]

Romeo waits for Juliet in Friar Laurence's cell…

Friar Laurence prays that their marriage won't bring trouble.

Love-devouring[6] death do what he dare — it is enough I may but call her mine.

Romeo answers that as long as he marries Juliet, he doesn't care what happens.

Here comes the lady. O, so light a foot will ne'er wear out the everlasting flint.[1]

Good even to my ghostly confessor.[2]

Just then, Juliet appears at the door.

Ah, Juliet, if the measure of thy joy be heaped like mine...

then sweeten with thy breath this neighbour air.[3]

Let rich music's tongue unfold the imagined happiness

that both receive in either by this dear encounter.[4]

My true love is grown to such excess I cannot sum up sum of half my wealth.[5]

Romeo steps forward, takes Juliet's hand lovingly, and looks deep into her eyes. Like Romeo, Juliet is overcome with emotion.

Come, come with me, and we will make short work.

The Friar knows time is of the essence, and promises to marry them as quickly as possible.

Romeo and Juliet are married.

1. so light… flint: Juliet walks so lightly she will never wear out the hard ground.   2: ghostly confessor: spiritual priest (who listens to confessions).   3. if the measure… air: if your joy is piled as high as mine, then sweeten the air with your words.
4. Let rich… encounter: Let your tongue speak words that talk of the happiness we both expect in getting married.
5. My true… wealth: My love for you has grown so great I can't add up half of how much I feel for you.

TROUBLE IN THE AIR

Mercutio and Benvolio are again in the piazza. It's a scorching hot day. Benvolio knows it's the sort of weather that brings trouble.

Mercutio laughs, saying Benvolio is as hot-tempered as anyone.

Benvolio steps back and gasps, pretending to be shocked by Mercutio's comments.

Benvolio spies a group of Capulets coming their way, led by Tybalt, Juliet's cousin.

Tybalt is still furious that Romeo attended Capulet's feast and is looking to fight a duel with Romeo.

Tybalt approaches Mercutio and Benvolio – he knows they are friends with Romeo.

Pointing to his sword, Mercutio makes fun of Tybalt – but there's a threat behind his teasing.

1. abroad: about. 3. consortest with: here it means 'are friends with'.
4. consort: here it means 'a band of musicians'. Mercutio deliberately misunderstands Tybalt to annoy him.
5. minstrels: hired musicians. 6. fiddlestick: here he means his sword.

Here all eyes gaze on us.

Well, peace be with you, sir. Here comes my man.

Romeo, the love I bear thee can afford no better reason than this:[1]

Thou art a villain.

Let them gaze. I will not budge for no man's pleasure, I.

Benvolio tries to stop the fight. Just then, Romeo arrives, so Tybalt leaves Mercutio alone.

Tybalt turns and challenges Romeo.

Villain am I none. Therefore farewell. I see thou knowest me not.

Boy, this shall not excuse the injuries that thou hast done me.

Good Capulet, which name I tender as dearly as mine own, be satisfied.

Therefore turn and draw.

Romeo turns and is ready to leave when Tybalt grabs his shoulder and spins him around.

Romeo wants to explain he has just married Juliet – but he can't. Now that he's related to Tybalt, he has no wish to fight him.

Tybalt, you ratcatcher, will you walk?[2]

What wouldst thou have with me?

They fight…

Good King of Cats, nothing but one of your nine lives.[3]

I am for you!

Tybalt is ready to leave Romeo alone when hot-headed Mercutio, disgusted that Romeo is not defending himelf, draws his sword and steps towards Tybalt, who rises to the bait.

1. The love I... than this: I can't say any better than this.   2. will you walk: do you refuse to fight?
3. nine lives: cats are often said to have 'nine lives' because of their good survival skills.

THE DUEL

They cut and thrust…

Desperate to stop the fight, Romeo steps between the two men.

Seeing his opportunity, Tybalt thrusts under Romeo's arm.

Tybalt stabs Mercutio, who staggers back, clutching at the wound in his chest.

As Romeo supports the wounded Mercutio in his arms, Benvolio runs over to help.

Mercutio blames Romeo for getting in the way.

Benvolio drags Mercutio to a nearby house where he can lie down until the doctor comes.

Romeo blames himself for the fight and Mercutio's fatal wound.

1. Hold: Stop.   2. A plague… houses: A curse on both Montagues and Capulets.
3. a scratch: Mercutio is pretending it's not a bad wound.   4: worms' meat: a corpse.   5. very: true.
140   6. My friend… behalf: My friend has got this deadly injury because of me.

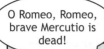
O Romeo, Romeo, brave Mercutio is dead!

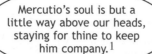
Mercutio's soul is but a little way above our heads, staying for thine to keep him company.[1]

Either thou, or I, or both must go with him!

A minute later, Benvolio comes rushing out of the house, with grim news.

Romeo sees that Tybalt is still standing nearby. His blood boils. Drawing his sword, he attacks.

Romeo, away, be gone! The Prince will doom thee death[2] if thou art taken.

O, I am fortune's fool!

Benvolio, who began this bloody fray?[3]

Romeo runs Tybalt through with his sword and kills him.

Benvolio warns Romeo the Prince will execute him, so Romeo runs away.

Soon after, the Prince arrives, along with Lords Montague and Capulet and their wives.

Romeo, he cries aloud, 'Hold, friends! Friends, part!' This is the truth, or let Benvolio die.

Romeo slew[4] Tybalt; Romeo must not live.

And for that offence immediately we do exile[5] him hence.

Benvolio explains that Romeo tried to stop the fighting, and only attacked Tybalt in revenge for Mercutio's death.

Lady Capulet says they can't trust Benvolio as he is related to Romeo. She wants bloody revenge.

The Prince, sad that his relative Mercutio has died, decides to banish Romeo from the city.

1. Mercutio... company: Mercutio's soul has not gone to heaven because he is waiting to see Tybalt killed in revenge.
2. doom thee death: condemn you to death.   3. fray: brawl.   4. slew: killed.   5. exile: banish.

BANISHED!

Meanwhile...

Come, loving, black-browed[1] night, give me my Romeo.

Juliet is in her room, alone. She can't wait for night – and her beloved Romeo – to arrive.

Why dost thou wring thy hands?

He's killed, he's dead.

Hearing footsteps, Juliet jumps up in excitement – Romeo will soon be with her. But the Nurse brings terrible news...

If he be slain, say 'Ay', if not, say 'No'.

O Tybalt, the best friend I had.

Juliet is stunned – she thinks the Nurse is talking about Romeo.

Juliet is still confused.

Is Romeo slaughtered, and is Tybalt dead? My dearest cousin, and my dearer lord?[2]

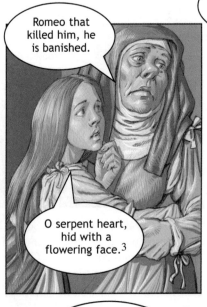

Romeo that killed him, he is banished.

O serpent heart, hid with a flowering face.[3]

That villain cousin would have killed my husband.

At first Juliet blames Romeo, but then she realises he may have had no choice.

I'll find Romeo to comfort you. He is hid at Laurence' cell.

'Romeo is banished': To speak that word is father, mother, Tybalt, Romeo, Juliet, all slain, all dead.

Give this ring to my true knight and bid him come to take his last farewell.

Juliet weeps as she realises she may never see Romeo again – for her, a fate worse than death.

The Nurse hands Juliet the rope ladder and promises to fetch Romeo. In return, Juliet hands Nurse her ring as a token for Romeo.

1. black-browed: dark.　2. lord: husband.　3: serpent... face: Juliet is comparing Romeo to a snake hiding in beautiful flowers – he has deceived her.

142

Father, what news?

Ha! Banishment! Be merciful, say 'death'.

This is dear mercy.[1]

Hence from Verona thou art banished.

'Tis torture, not mercy.

Meanwhile, Romeo is hiding in Friar Laurence's cell.

When Romeo groans in despair, the Friar tries to comfort him.

I come from Lady Juliet. For Juliet's sake, rise and stand!

They hear a knock. Terrified, Romeo hides himself. The Nurse enters and sees Romeo cowering.

Spak'st thou[2] of Juliet? How is it with her? Doth she not think me an old[3] murderer?

O, she says nothing, sir, but weeps and weeps.

In desperation, Romeo tries to stab himself with a knife, but the Nurse snatches the dagger away.

Art thou a man? Thy tears are womanish.

The Friar tells Romeo to pull himself together – he has a plan!

The Friar explains…

How well my comfort is revived by this![5]

The Friar will arrange for Romeo to go to Mantua[4] and will try to persuade the Prince to pardon him. Romeo can spend the night with Juliet, but must leave early to avoid capture. Romeo cheers up at the thought of seeing Juliet.

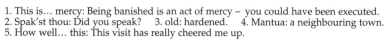

1. This is… mercy: Being banished is an act of mercy – you could have been executed.
2. Spak'st thou: Did you speak?   3. old: hardened.   4. Mantua: a neighbouring town.
5. How well… this: This visit has really cheered me up.

A Sad Farewell

Unaware that Juliet has married Romeo, Lord Capulet is busy arranging Juliet's wedding with Paris. Meanwhile, Romeo has climbed up into Juliet's room to spend the night with her.

Morning breaks...

But time passes quickly, and soon Romeo must leave. He climbs out of Juliet's window.

Juliet goes back into her room, just as her mother enters. Afraid that she may never see Romeo again, she can't stop crying.

Lady Capulet thinks that Juliet's tears are for her murdered cousin.

Lady Capulet promises revenge for Tybalt's death. Juliet has to pretend that she wants vengeance too.

1. A Thursday: On Thursday.   2. Yond: Yonder, over there.   3. Let me... wilt it: I don't mind being caught and executed if that's what you want.   4. The day is broke: It is daybreak.   5. Then, window... out: Then let the light in and let my beloved leave.   6. Evermore... death: Are you still crying over Tybalt's death?   7. behold: see.
8. I... dead: Juliet's words have a double meaning – she's also saying 'As long as Romeo lives, I can't get enough of him.'

Marry, my child, early next Thursday morn.

I will not marry yet. And when I do, I swear, it shall be Romeo, whom you know I hate,[1] rather than Paris.

Lady Capulet breaks the news that her father wants Juliet to marry Paris – in just three days. Juliet bluntly refuses, saying it is too soon after Tybalt's death.

Hang thee, young baggage![2] Disobedient wretch!

I tell thee what – Get thee to church a Thursday or never after look me in the face.

When Lord Capulet hears Juliet's reply, he flies into a rage.

Lord Capulet disowns Juliet.

You are too hot.[4]

And you be mine I'll give you to my friend; and you be not[3] – hang! Beg! Starve! Die in the streets!

For by my soul I'll never acknowledge thee.

O Nurse, how can this be prevented? Hast thou not a word of joy?

After her parents leave, Juliet asks her Nurse for advice.

Romeo is banished. I think you are happy with this second match, for it excels your first.

But instead of giving Juliet hope, the Nurse suggests she forget all about Romeo and marry Paris instead. Juliet is shocked.

Speakst thou from the heart?

And from my soul too.

O most wicked fiend! I'll to the Friar to know his remedy.[5] If all else fail, myself have power to die.

Juliet pretends to agree, but as the Nurse leaves, she decides to go to Friar Laurence for help instead.

1. And when I do... hate: Juliet is making it sound like she'd rather marry anyone but Paris, when actually all she wants is Romeo.   2. baggage: immoral woman.   3. And you be mine... be not: If you're really my daughter, I'll give you to Paris, but if you're not...   4. hot: angry.   5. remedy: solution, plan.

145

Friar Laurence's Plan

On Thursday, sir? The time is very short.

Now, sir, her father counts it dangerous that she do give her sorrow too much sway,

and in his wisdom hastes our marriage.

Juliet hurries to see Friar Laurence, not knowing that Paris is visiting the Friar to arrange their marriage. But the Friar is trying to delay the ceremony, knowing full well he has already married Juliet to Romeo.

Paris explains that Juliet's father is keen to speed up the marriage as he is worried that Juliet is so upset at Tybalt's death.

I wish I knew not why it should be slowed.

Happily met, my lady and my wife!

The Friar tries to look pleased for Paris, but is secretly worried about what will happen when Lord Capulet finds out about Juliet's marriage to Romeo.

At that moment, Juliet appears, looking flustered. Paris is delighted that she has turned up, thinking it a happy coincidence.

That may be, sir, when I may be a wife.

That 'may be' must be, love, on Thursday next.

What must be, shall be.

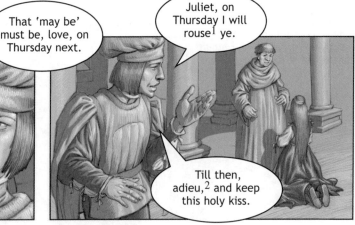

Juliet, on Thursday I will rouse[1] ye.

Till then, adieu,[2] and keep this holy kiss.

Juliet wants to talk to the Friar about Romeo but can't say a thing with Paris there. Paris is eager to talk about the wedding, but Juliet is reluctant.

Finally, to get rid of Paris, Juliet pretends she has come to make her confession. Paris leaves so she can be alone with the Friar.

1. rouse: wake up.   2. adieu: farewell.

O, shut the door and when thou hast done so, come weep with me — past hope, past cure, past help!

If in thy wisdom thou canst not help... with this knife I'll help it presently.[1]

Hold, daughter, I do spy a kind of hope.

Once Paris has gone, Juliet bursts into tears.

Juliet is so upset that she threatens to kill herself with a dagger.

The Friar calms Juliet down and takes the knife from her.

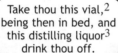

Take thou this vial,[2] being then in bed, and this distilling liquor[3] drink thou off.

When the bridegroom in the morning comes to rouse thee from thy bed, there art thou dead.[4]

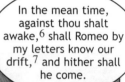

In the mean time, against thou shalt awake,[6] shall Romeo by my letters know our drift,[7] and hither shall he come.

The Friar reveals his plan: the night before her wedding to Paris, she must swallow a potion that will make her look dead.

When Paris finds her everyone will think she's dead and she'll be buried in the family vault.[5]

When the potion wears off, the Friar and Romeo will be waiting. Then Juliet and Romeo can leave Verona and start a new life.

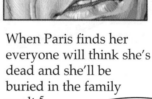

Give me, give me! O tell not me of fear!

I'll send a Friar with speed to Mantua, with my letters to thy lord.

Love, give me strength! Farewell, dear Father.[8]

Juliet takes the vial. The Friar warns her the potion is not for the faint-hearted.

The Friar promises that he will send a messenger to Romeo so that he will know the plan.

Juliet thanks him and leaves, clutching the potion in her hand.

1. with this knife... presently: if you can't help me, I'll stab myself with this knife.   2. vial: bottle.
3. distilling liquor: drink that spreads through a body.   4. there art thou dead: you will seem dead.
5. vault: tomb.   6. against... awake: to be ready when you wake.   7. drift: plan.   8. Father: Catholic priest.

THE VIAL OF POTION

Juliet returns home. Falling to her knees, she pretends she is happy to marry Paris.

At this, Lord Capulet decides to move the wedding ahead one day. He tells the Nurse that Juliet is to be married the next day!

Later, as she gets ready for bed, Juliet asks the Nurse if she can be alone.

Juliet, still dressed, sits alone on her bed. Scared but determined, she takes out the vial of potion. She is terrified that it might kill her rather than just make her sleep deeply.

Juliet is worried she might wake up in the tomb alone, next to Tybalt's body. Despite this, she drinks the potion.

Downstairs, unaware of what is happening, Lord and Lady Capulet are busy preparing for the wedding feast.

1. Pardon… by you: Please forgive me, from now on I'll do as you say.
2. Make haste: Hurry up!

The next morning…

The potion does its work. Juliet is in a very deep sleep when the Nurse comes to wake her.

When the Nurse feels Juliet's stiff, cold body, she screams in horror.

Juliet's mother and father rush into her room. They're shocked by what they find – everyone thinks Juliet is dead.

Paris and the Friar enter the room. Paris looks on in horror as Lord and Lady Capulet weep over Juliet's body.

Playing his part, the Friar gently persuades Capulet to place Juliet's body in the family vault. So far the plan is working well.

But tragedy strikes! The Friar's messenger never reaches Romeo, as a plague prevents him from entering Mantua. Romeo knows nothing of the Friar's plan! He hears from his servant Balthasar only that Juliet is dead. Romeo can't believe his ears.

Romeo makes plans to return to Verona. He will visit Juliet in the tomb that night.

1. Ready to... return: Ready to be buried. 2. Capel: the Capulet family.
3. Is it e'en so?: Can this really be true? 4. stars: fate, destiny.

149

THE TOMB

"Well, Juliet, I will lie with thee tonight."

After Balthasar leaves…

Romeo breaks down and weeps for Juliet. He decides to kill himself rather than live without her.

Romeo visits an apothecary[1] to buy some poison.

"Hold, there is forty ducats.[2] Let me have a dram[3] of poison."

"My poverty, but not my will[4] consents."

"Come, cordial[5] and not poison, go with me to Juliet's grave."

"I pay thy poverty and not thy will."

"Unhappy fortune! Friar John, go hence."

"Get me an iron crow[6] and bring it straight unto my cell."

The Apothecary knows the law forbids him from selling poison, but he is poor and cannot resist Romeo's gold.

Poison in hand, Romeo heads to see Juliet, even though he has been banished from Verona.

Meanwhile, Friar Laurence hears that Romeo never received his message. He realises he must free Juliet from the tomb.

"Whistle then to me, as signal that thou hearest something approach."

That night…

Paris visits the tomb where Juliet's body lies. He tells his servant to warn him if anyone else enters the churchyard.

"What cursed foot wanders this way tonight?"

As Paris lays flowers on Juliet's tomb, he hears his page whistling: someone is coming!

It is Romeo, walking towards the tomb with a torch and a crowbar. He has ordered his servant Balthasar to leave him alone.

1. apothecary: someone who sells drugs or medicines.   2. ducats: gold coins.   3. dram: small amount.
4. will: conscience, sense of right and wrong.   5. cordial: medicine – it will relieve Romeo's pain.
6. crow: crowbar, a hooked iron bar used to force open doors.

As Romeo forces open the tomb door with his crowbar, Paris steps forward. When he recognises Romeo, he is furious.

Romeo tries to persuade Paris to leave him alone. But Paris refuses, so Romeo draws his sword and they fight.

As Paris lies dying, he has one final request.

Romeo carries Paris's body into the tomb and lays it down. In the flickering torchlight, he sees Juliet's body lying nearby. He gazes at her face one last time.

Though Romeo is surprised by Juliet's red cheeks and lips, he does not realise she is still alive.

1. Condemned… thee: You criminal, I arrest you.   2. tempt… man: don't push me as I'm desperate.
3. Have at thee: Take that!   4. Death… beauty: Death has taken your breath away, but not your beauty.
5. Beauty… there: Your lips and cheeks are still rosy – you haven't turned pale in death.

ALL ARE PUNISHED

Romeo! O pale! Who else?

What, Paris too? And steeped in blood?

Where is my Romeo?

Arriving at the tomb, the Friar meets Balthasar and hears that Romeo has got there first.

He notices a pool of blood from a fight. Dashing inside, he finds Romeo's pale body and Paris's bloody corpse.

Just then, Juliet awakes. The effects of the potion have worn off. Not seeing Romeo's dead body, she asks the Friar what has happened.

Come, come away. Thy husband in thy bosom there lies dead.

I will not away.

O churl![1] Drunk all, and left no friendly drop to help me after?[2]

Thy lips are warm!

Hearing the Prince's men outside, the Friar tries to lead Juliet out of the tomb, but she refuses.

While the Friar makes his escape, Juliet sees the vial of poison in Romeo's hand.

Deciding to join Romeo in death, Juliet kisses his lips, hoping some of the poison will rub off.

O happy dagger!

This is thy sheath;[3] there rust, and let me die.

Go, tell the Prince. Run to the Capulets! Raise up the Montagues!

The Prince's men are just outside, so Juliet decides to act quickly. Seizing Romeo's dagger, she plunges it into her chest and dies. Just then, the soldiers enter the tomb.

1. churl: a person with bad manners.
2. Drunk all...after?: You drank all the poison and left none to help me follow you?
3. This is...sheath: When I plunge this dagger into me, my body will become its sheath (covering).

Hold him in safety until the Prince comes hither.

Sovereign,[1] here lies the County Paris slain; and Romeo dead; and Juliet.

By now it is dawn.

O heavens! O wife, look how our daughter bleeds!

Two guards bring in the Friar and Balthasar, having captured them in the graveyard.

When the Prince arrives, along with Lord and Lady Capulet, the soldiers explain what has happened.

Lady Capulet screams and runs to hold Juliet, while Lord Capulet looks on in horror.

My wife is dead tonight! Grief of my son's exile hath stopped her breath.

Romeo, there dead, was husband to that Juliet; I married them.

This letter he early bid me give his father.

Lord Montague enters, bringing news that his wife collapsed and died when she heard Romeo was banished.

The Friar explains all: Romeo and Juliet's secret marriage, the potion, and why Romeo killed himself when the letter did not reach him.

Balthasar tells how Paris and Romeo came to fight. He hands the Prince a letter Romeo wrote to his father.

Capulet, Montague, see what a scourge is laid upon your hate.[2] All are punished.

For never was a story of more woe than this of Juliet and her Romeo.

As rich shall Romeo by his lady lie — poor sacrifices of our enmity.[3]

After reading the letter, the Prince shames Lords Capulet and Montague for the tragedy they have brought upon themselves.

Montague and Capulet agree to end their family feud and erect a statue of the two lovers as a memorial.

The End

1. Sovereign: Ruler, lord.
2. see what… hate: see what a tragedy your hatred has brought.
3. poor sacrifices… enmity: our hatred cost their lives.

A MIDSUMMER NIGHT'S DREAM

William Shakespeare

Illustrated by

Penko Gelev

Retold by

Ian Graham

Series created and designed by

David Salariya

*Ancient Greece:
The palace of Theseus,
Duke of Athens*

Duke Theseus is preparing for his marriage to Hippolyta, Queen of the Amazons, a race of warrior women. There are four days to go before the wedding, and Theseus plans to fill the time with lavish entertainment.

CHARACTERS

Theseus, Duke of Athens

Hippolyta, Queen of the Amazons

Oberon, King of the Fairies

Titania, Queen of the Fairies

Puck, or Robin Goodfellow, Oberon's jester

Egeus, a nobleman

Hermia, Egeus's daughter, in love with Lysander

Demetrius, a young courtier, in love with Hermia

Lysander, a young courtier, also in love with Hermia

Helena, in love with Demetrius

Peter Quince, a carpenter

Nick Bottom, a weaver

Francis Flute, a bellows-mender

Robin Starveling, a tailor

Tom Snout, a tinker

Snug, a joiner

Philostrate, Theseus's Master of the Revels*

Peaseblossom

Cobweb

Moth

Mustardseed

Four fairies who are servants of Titania

Master of the Revels: official in charge of court entertainments.

An Angry Visitor

Theseus's palace, Athens

Now, fair Hippolyta, our nuptial hour draws on apace.[1]

Theseus is looking forward to his wedding to Hippolyta.

Theseus won Hippolyta in battle, but he vows to marry her with great celebrations and entertainments.

Full of vexation[2] come I, with complaint against my child, my daughter Hermia.

This man hath my consent to marry her.

Egeus arrives at the palace and asks Theseus to punish his daughter for refusing to marry Demetrius.

Egeus accuses Lysander of stealing his daughter's heart.

As she is mine, I may dispose of her[3]...

What say you, Hermia? Demetrius is a worthy gentleman.

This man hath bewitched the bosom of my child.

...either to this gentleman, or to her death.

So is Lysander.

Demetrius — I'll avouch it to his head[4] — made love to[5] Nedar's daughter Helena, and won her soul.

Fit your fancies to your father's will[6] —

— or else the law of Athens yields you up to death, or to a vow of single life.[7]

I must confess that I have heard so much.

1. our nuptial hour draws on apace: our wedding approaches fast.
2. Full of vexation: Angry.   3. dispose of her: decide who is to have her.   4. I'll avouch it to his head: I'll say it to his face.
5. made love to: courted.   6. Fit . . . will: Agree to do what your father wants (marry Demetrius).   7. a vow of single life: life as a nun in a convent.

RUNNING AWAY

Lysander suggests to Hermia that they marry outside Athens, where Athenian law does not apply.

The course of true love never did run smooth.[1]

I have a widow aunt.

From Athens is her house remote seven leagues.[2]

There, gentle Hermia, may I marry thee.

Lysander asks Hermia to meet him in the wood the next night.

Steal forth[3] thy father's house tomorrow night; and in the wood, a league without[4] the town, there will I stay[5] for thee.

My good Lysander, I swear to thee... truly I will meet with thee.

Hermia agrees to run away with Lysander.

God speed fair Helena!

Call you me fair? Demetrius loves *your* fair.[6]

Were the world mine, Demetrius being bated,[7] the rest I'd give to be to you translated.[8]

O, teach me how you look, and with what art you sway the motion of Demetrius' heart.

Helena bemoans the fact that Demetrius loves Hermia and not her.

Helena would give anything to change places with Hermia. Helena asks Hermia for the secret to winning Demetrius's love.

1. The course of true love never did run smooth: Those who are in love always face problems.
2. remote seven leagues: seven leagues (about 35 kilometres) away.   3. Steal forth: Sneak away from.   4. without: outside.   5. stay: wait.   6. your fair: your beauty.   7. Demetrius being bated: except for Demetrius.   8. to be to you translated: to be transformed into you.

Whatever Hermia does to discourage Demetrius, he still loves her.

I frown upon him; yet he loves me still.

O that your frowns would teach my smiles such skill!

The more I hate, the more he follows me.

The more I love, the more he hateth me.

His folly,[1] Helena, is no fault of mine.

Hermia protests that she does nothing to attract Demetrius.

Take comfort: he no more shall see my face; Lysander and myself will fly this place.

Through Athens' gates have we devis'd[2] to steal.

Lysander and Hermia tell Helena of their plan to run away.

Farewell, sweet playfellow; pray thou for us, and good luck grant thee thy Demetrius!

Hermia hopes that when she leaves, Demetrius may once again love Helena.

Ere Demetrius look'd on Hermia's eyne,[3] he hail'd down oaths[4] that he was only mine.

Helena remembers how Demetrius loved her before he saw Hermia.

I will go tell him of fair Hermia's flight.

Helena plans to win Demetrius back.

1. His folly: His foolishness.   2. devis'd: planned.   3. Ere Demetrius look'd on Hermia's eyne: Before Demetrius looked into Hermia's eyes.   4. he hail'd down oaths: he swore.

THE PLAYERS MEET

Peter Quince, a carpenter, has written a play to perform for the Duke and Duchess after their wedding.

1. scroll: list.   2. interlude: a short play put on between other entertainments.   3. Marry: A word that means something like 'indeed' or 'now then'.   4. lamentable: very sad. Quince doesn't seem to know what 'comedy' means.
5. tyrant: cruel ruler.   6. most gallant: very bravely.   7. to play a woman: In Shakespeare's time it was normal for female characters to be played by boys.   8. monstrous little: tiny.

Robin Starveling, you must play Thisbe's mother.

Tom Snout, the tinker? You, Pyramus' father. Myself, Thisbe's father.

Snug, the joiner, you the lion's part.

Have you the lion's part written? Pray you, if it be, give it me; for I am slow of study.

You may do it extempore,[1] for it is nothing but roaring.

Let me play the lion too. I will roar, that I will do any man's heart good to hear me.

You would fright the Duchess and the ladies.

I will aggravate[2] my voice so, that I will roar you as gently as any sucking dove.

You can play no part but Pyramus: for Pyramus is a sweet-faced man.

Snug worries about learning his lines, but there are none. All he has to do is roar.

Quince tells Bottom that Pyramus is a very handsome man. Flattered, Bottom agrees to play only Pyramus.

Quince urges the actors to learn their parts well.

They agree to rehearse the play in the wood, where no-one will see them.

Masters, here are your parts; and I am to entreat you, request you, and desire you, to con them[3] by tomorrow night.

Meet me in the palace wood, a mile without[4] the town, by moonlight; there will we rehearse.

1. do it extempore: make it up as you go.
2. aggravate: make stronger. Bottom means to say the opposite – 'I will mitigate (soften) my voice' – but he chooses the wrong word.
3. con them: learn them by heart.
4. without: outside.

OBERON PLOTS

Meanwhile, in the wood:

How now, spirit!

Puck, who serves Oberon, meets a fairy who serves Titania, the fairy queen.

The King doth keep his revels[1] here tonight; take heed the Queen come not within his sight.

Puck warns the fairy to keep Titania and Oberon apart, because they are bound to quarrel.

She as her attendant hath a lovely boy, stol'n from an Indian king — and jealous Oberon would have the child.

They are aguing over a servant boy.

You are that shrewd and knavish sprite[2] call'd Robin Goodfellow.

Thou speak'st aright.[3]

The fairy recognises Puck and calls him by his other name.

Ill met[4] by moonlight, proud Titania.

What, jealous Oberon!

The King and Queen of Fairies meet by chance in the wood and immediately start arguing.

Your warrior love to Theseus must be wedded.

I know thy love to Theseus.

Titania accuses Oberon of being in love with Hippolyta. Oberon accuses Titania of loving Theseus.

I do but beg a little changeling boy[5] to be my henchman.[6]

His mother was a votress[7] of my order.

But she, being mortal, of that boy did die;[8] and for her sake do I rear up her boy.

Oberon asks for the child, but Titania refuses.

Give me that boy.

Not for thy fairy kingdom.

Fairies, away!

164   1. keep his revels: hold a party.   2. shrewd and knavish sprite: mischievous and roguish fairy.   3. Thou speak'st aright: You are correct.   4. Ill met: You are unwelcome.   5. changeling boy: human boy stolen by the fairies.   6. henchman: page of honour.   7. votress: devoted follower.   8. of that boy did die: died giving birth to the boy.

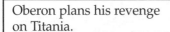
Oberon plans his revenge on Titania.

Well, go thy way; thou shalt not from[1] this grove till I torment thee for this injury.[2]

Once I sat upon a promontory,[3] and heard a mermaid on a dolphin's back.

I remember.

Oberon reminds Puck of something he saw once.

I saw Cupid all arm'd.[4]

A certain aim he took, and loos'd his love-shaft[5] smartly from his bow.

He remembers seeing Cupid, the god of love, firing an arrow.

It fell upon a little western flower.

The arrow landed on a flower.

Fetch me that flower.

The juice of it, on sleeping eyelids laid, will make a man or woman madly dote upon[6] the next live creature that it sees.

Oberon sends Puck away to find the magic flower.

I'll put a girdle round about the earth[7] in forty minutes.

I'll watch Titania when she is asleep, and drop the liquor of it in her eyes.

The next thing then she waking looks upon — she shall pursue it with the soul of love!

I'll make her render up her page to me.[8]

Puck promises to be quick.

Oberon plans to use the juice of the magic flower on Titania.

He'll trick Titania into giving her Indian boy to him.

1. Thou shalt not from: You shall not leave.   2. injury: insult.   3. promontory: headland.   4. Cupid all arm'd: the god of love, armed with a bow.   5. love-shaft: Cupid's arrow, which makes its victims fall in love.   6. dote upon: fall in love with.   7. I'll put a girdle round about the earth: I'll circle the world.   8. render up her page to me: let me have her servant boy.

Seeking Hermia

Demetrius searches the wood for Lysander and Hermia, but can't find them.

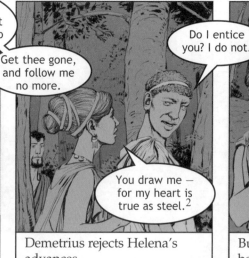

Demetrius rejects Helena's advances.

But Helena will not be put off.

Demetrius doesn't want Helena to follow him.

Demetrius threatens to leave Helena to the wild animals in the wood.

Demetrius threatens to hurt Helena himself unless she leaves him alone.

Helena welcomes death if it is at the hand of her love, Demetrius.

1. they were stol'n unto this wood: they went unseen to this wood.   2. You draw me – for my heart is true as steel: You attract me like a magnet, as if my heart were made of steel.   3. I am your spaniel: Treat me like a pet dog.
4. fawn on you: show you great affection.   5. in my respect: in my eyes.   6. brakes: dense undergrowth.

Ere he do leave this grove[1]...

...thou shalt fly him, and he shall seek thy love.

Oberon plans to punish Demetrius for his rudeness.

Hast thou the flower there?[2]

Ay, there it is.

Puck returns with the magic flower.

I know a bank where the wild thyme blows.[3] There sleeps Titania sometime of the night.

Take thou some of it, and seek through this grove. A sweet Athenian lady is in love with a disdainful[4] youth.

Anoint[5] his eyes; but do it when the next thing he espies may be the lady.

And with the juice of this I'll streak her eyes, and make her full of hateful fantasies.

Oberon sends Puck to look for Helena.

Thou shalt know the man by the Athenian garments he hath on.

Effect it with some care,[6] that he may prove more fond on[7] her than she upon her love.

Fear not, my lord, your servant shall do so.

Oberon tells Puck how to recognise Demetrius by his clothes.

1. Ere he do leave this grove: Before he leaves this wood.   2. Hast thou the flower there?: Do you have the flower?
3. blows: flowers.   4. disdainful: scornful.   5. anoint: smear.   6. Effect it with some care: Do it carefully.
7. fond on: in love with.

Lost in the Wood

The fairies sing until Titania falls asleep.

Oberon squeezes magic flower juice onto Titania's eyelids. She will love the next person she sees. Oberon hopes it will be a monster!

Lysander and Hermia stop to rest, because Lysander has forgotten the way to his aunt's house.

They lie down to sleep – not together as Lysander wishes, but apart.

Puck is still searching for Demetrius.

He mistakes Lysander and Hermia for Demetrius and Helena.

Puck squeezes some juice from the magic flower onto Lysander's eyelids.

1. offices: duties.   2. What thou seest when thou dost wake, do it for thy true-love take: Whatever you see when you awake, you will fall in love with it.   3. you faint: you're very tired.   4. troth: truth.   5. churl: ill-mannered person. (Puck thinks he is speaking to Demetrius, who has insulted Helena.)   6. owe: possess.

Meanwhile:

Do not haunt me thus.[1]

Stay, though thou kill me, sweet Demetrius!

Demetrius is still trying to get away from Helena.

O wilt thou darkling leave me?[2] Do not so.

Stay, on thy peril; I alone will go.

Helena begs Demetrius not to leave her alone in the dark wood.

Lysander, on the ground? Dead, or asleep? I see no blood, no wound...

Good sir, awake.

She discovers Lysander on the ground.

Run through fire I will for thy sweet sake!

Yet Hermia still loves you; then be content.

Content with Hermia? No! Not Hermia, but Helena I love.

Lysander awakes — and falls in love with Helena the moment he sees her.

You do me wrong, in such disdainful manner me to woo.[3]

She thinks he is making fun of her.

Hermia, sleep thou there; and never mayst thou come Lysander near!

Help me, Lysander, help me! Do thy best to pluck this crawling serpent[4] from my breast!

Lysander, no longer in love with Hermia, leaves without her.

Hermia wakens from a nightmare. She has dreamt that a snake is attacking her.

Lysander! What, remov'd?[5] Lysander! lord!

Either death or you I'll find immediately.

Shocked to discover that Lysander has gone without her, she sets off to find him.

1. Do not haunt me thus: Don't hang around me all the time like this.   2. O wilt thou darkling leave me? Will you leave me in the dark?   3. You do me wrong, in such disdainful manner me to woo: You treat me badly, to pretend so cruelly that you love me.   4. serpent: snake.   5. remov'd: gone.

169

MAKING AN ASS OF BOTTOM

The actors meet in the wood.

Bottom voices his worries about the play.

He suggests a way to solve the play's problems – write a prologue.[3]

Snout thinks of another problem.

Someone must play the Moon...

...and the wall that keeps the lovers apart.

An actor will hold his fingers apart to make a hole that Pyramus and Thisbe can talk through.

1. pat: perfectly.   2. cannot abide: cannot bear. Bottom thinks the audience will be frightened, thinking the action on stage is real.   3. prologue: a speech given to an audience before a play, telling them what to expect. The actor who makes this speech is also called the Prologue.   4. device: plan.   5. afeard: afraid.   6. to present the person of Moonshine: to represent the Moon.   7. the chink of a wall: a crack in a wall.

Puck discovers the actors in the wood.

Pyramus, played by Bottom, hears a voice offstage.

When Bottom returns, Puck has worked mischievous magic on him!

Titania is awakened by Bottom's singing.

Bewitched by the magic flower juice, she instantly falls in love with him.

Titania orders her fairies to look after Bottom.

1. hempen homespuns: people wearing clothes home-made from hemp; in other words, country bumpkins.
2. Hark: Listen.   3. knavery: wicked trick.   4. I pray thee: I beg you.

MISTAKEN IDENTITY

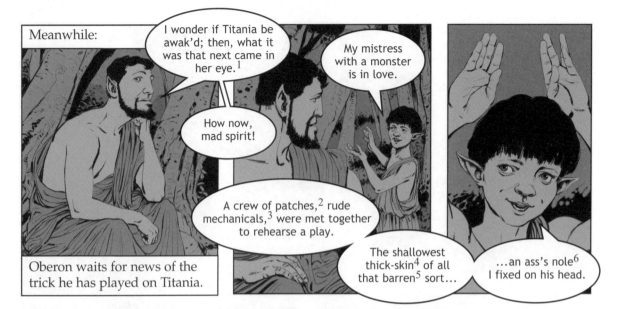

Oberon waits for news of the trick he has played on Titania.

Oberon is pleased with Puck's work.

Puck says he has used the magic flower juice on Demetrius.

Puck realises that he has put the magic juice on the wrong man!

1. what it was that next came in her eye: what she saw when she woke.   2. crew of patches: group of fools.
3. rude mechanicals: uneducated workmen.   4. thick-skin: brutish fellow.   5. barren: empty   6. nole: head.
7. latch'd: moistened.   8. as I did bid thee do: as I asked you to do.

Hermia suspects that Demetrius has killed Lysander out of jealousy.

Demetrius denies killing Lysander.

Hermia storms off and Demetrius lies down to sleep.

Puck must find Helena.

This time, the magic flower juice will make Demetrius love Helena.

Helena approaches, followed by Lysander.

1. rebuke: scold, tell off.   2. slain: killed.   3. stol'n away: crept away unnoticed.   4. carcass: dead body.
5. You spend . . . misprised mood: You are getting carried away by your mistaken anger.   6. vein: temper.
7. look: make sure that.   8. fond pageant: foolish antics.

RIVALS IN LOVE

Helena refuses to believe that Lysander loves her.

Lysander says he was mistaken when he thought he loved Hermia.

Demetrius awakes and declares his love for Helena, but she thinks he is mocking her.

Now neither of them is interested in Hermia.

Helena scolds the two men for making fun of her.

1. in scorn: not seriously.   2. vow: promise.
3. nymph: a spirit of nature, a beautiful maiden.
4. bent: determined.
5. do me thus much injury: insult me so much.
6. ere: before.

Hermia finds Lysander by following the sound of his voice.

Hermia still doesn't understand why Lysander left her alone in the wood.

Helena is convinced that the other three are playing a cruel joke on her.

1. yonder: over there.   2. press: force, compel.   3. engilds: decorates with gold, makes more beautiful.
4. oes and eyes of light: stars.   5. conjoin'd: banded together.   6. in spite of me: against me.
7. Ay, do, . . . hold the sweet jest up: Go on then, keep it up, keep the joke going.

LOVE AND HATE

Demetrius and Lysander both pledge their love for Helena.

They are even ready to fight over her.

Hermia tries to stop them, but Lysander is furious.

Hermia accuses Helena of stealing Lysander's love.

Helen, I love thee, by my life, I do.

I say I love thee more than he can do.

If thou say so, withdraw[1] and prove it too.

Why are you grown so rude? What change is this, sweet love?

Hang off, thou cat, thou burr![2] Vile thing, let loose, or I will shake thee from me like a serpent.

Thy love? Out, tawny Tartar,[3] out!

Do you not jest?[4]

Be certain, nothing truer; 'tis no jest that I do hate thee, and love Helena.

You canker-blossom![5] Have you come by night and stol'n my love's heart from him?

1. withdraw: come away.   2. burr: a seed covered with hooks that sticks to clothes and animal fur. He means that she is clinging to him and won't let go.   3. tawny Tartar: dark-skinned barbarian. In Shakespeare's time, very pale skin was fashionable.   4. Do you not jest?: Surely you're joking?   5. canker-blossom: a grub that ruins a beautiful flower.

Only Helena's love for Demetrius stops her from leaving.

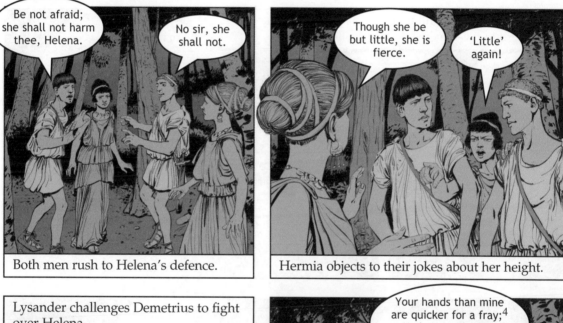

Both men rush to Helena's defence.

Hermia objects to their jokes about her height.

Lysander challenges Demetrius to fight over Helena.

1. Who is't that hinders you?: Who is it that stops you leaving?   2. A foolish heart . . . behind: According to Elizabethan poetry, when you are in love your heart stays with your loved one.   3. to try . . . Helena: to find out which of us has most right to Helena.   4. fray: fight.

KEEPING THE PEACE

Oberon isn't sure whether Puck caused the chaos by accident or design.

This is thy negligence. Still thou mistak'st – or else committ'st thy knaveries wilfully.[1]

Believe me, king of shadows,[2] I mistook.

Did not you tell me I should know the man by the Athenian garments he had on?

Puck was told to give the magic juice to an Athenian – and that's what he did.

Lead these testy[3] rivals so astray as one come not within another's way.

Now he must keep Lysander and Demetrius apart so they can't fight.

He must tire them out till they fall asleep, then use another magic herb to reverse the effect of the flower juice.

From each other look thou lead them thus...

...till o'er their brows death-counterfeiting sleep with leaden legs and batty wings doth creep.[4]

Then crush this herb into Lysander's eye.

I'll to my queen, and beg her Indian boy; and then I will her charmed eye release from monster's view, and all things shall be peace.

Meanwhile, Oberon will free Titania from her love of Bottom.

Up and down, up and down, I will lead them up and down.

Where art thou, proud Demetrius? Speak thou now.

Here, villain, drawn[5] and ready. Where art thou?

Puck confuses the lovers by mimicking their voices.

1. This is thy negligence . . . wilfully: This is your carelessness. You keep making mistakes – or else you played these tricks on purpose.   2. shadows: spirits.   3. testy: quarrelsome.   4. till o'er their brows . . . doth creep: until they are overcome by a deep, death-like sleep.   5. drawn: with a drawn sword.

Lysander! Thou runaway, thou coward, art thou fled?[1]

Thou coward! I'll whip thee with a rod; he is defil'd[2] that draws a sword on thee.

When I come where he calls, then he is gone.

The villain is much lighter-heel'd[3] than I.

Lysander, puzzled, gives up the chase and lies down to rest.

Come, thou gentle day. I'll find Demetrius, and revenge this spite.[4]

Where art thou now?

Ho, ho, ho! Coward, why com'st thou not?

Come hither;[5] I am here.

Shine, comforts,[6] from the east, that I may back to Athens by daylight.

Helena yearns for daybreak, to find her way back to Athens.

I can no further crawl, no further go. Here will I rest me till the break of day.

Hermia is exhausted.

On the ground
Sleep sound;
I'll apply
To your eye,
Gentle lover, remedy.

When thou wak'st
Thou tak'st
True delight
In the sight
Of thy former lady's[7] eye.

Puck sings as he applies the herb to Lysander's eyelids.

1. art thou fled?: have you run away?   2. defil'd: disgraced.   3. lighter-heel'd: faster.   4. spite: bad luck.
5. Come hither: Come here.   6. comforts: reassuring daylight.   7. thy former lady: the lady you loved before (Hermia).   **179**

RIGHTING WRONGS

Come sit thee down upon this flowery bed,while I thy amiable[1] cheeks do coy[2]...

Titania dotes on Bottom. She makes her fairy servants pamper him.

Ready.

Where's Peaseblossom?

...and kiss thy fair large ears, my gentle joy.

Scratch my head, Peaseblossom.

Monsieur[3] Cobweb, kill me a red-hipped humble-bee[4] and bring me the honey-bag.

Where's Monsieur Mustardseed?

Wilt thou hear some music, my sweet love?

I have a reasonable good ear in music.[7]

Ready.

Help Cavalery[5] Cobweb[6] to scratch.

Say, sweet love, what thou desir'st to eat.

Methinks I have a great desire to a bottle of hay.[8]

I have an exposition[9] of sleep come upon me.

Bottom's tastes are those of a donkey.

Sleep thou, and I will wind thee in my arms. Fairies, be gone!

1. amiable: lovable.   2. coy: caress, stroke.   3. Monsieur: French for 'Mr' or 'Master'.   4. humble-bee: bumblebee.
5. Cavalery: *cavaliero*, an Italian word for a sprightly military man.   6. Cobweb: Shakespeare has forgotten that it is
Peaseblossom who is scratching Bottom's head.   7. good ear in music: Donkeys are famous for the unmusical sounds
that they make.   8. bottle of hay: bundle of hay.   9. exposition: He means 'disposition', an inclination or tendency.

Oberon has persuaded Titania to give him the changeling…

Welcome, good Robin.[1] Seest thou this sweet sight?

When I had at my pleasure taunted her, I then did ask of her her changeling child; which straight she gave me.

…and now prepares to release her from his spell.

And now I have the boy, I will undo this hateful imperfection of her eyes.

My Oberon! What visions have I seen! Methought I was enamour'd of an ass.[2]

There lies your love.

How came these things to pass?

Robin, take off this head.

Titania thinks she has been dreaming.

Come, my queen, take hands with me…

…and rock the ground[3] whereon these sleepers be.

Oberon and Titania dance.

Tell me how it came this night that I sleeping here was found with these mortals on the ground.

Titania still has no idea what happened to her.

1. Robin: Robin Goodfellow, Puck's other name.   2. enamour'd of an ass: in love with a donkey.   3. take hands with me, and rock the ground: dance with me.

ALL'S WELL

Theseus and Hippolyta are hunting in the wood.

Since we have the vaward of the day,[1] my love shall hear the music of my hounds.[2]

Hippolyta tells Theseus of a hunt she enjoyed in Crete.

Never did I hear such gallant chiding.[3]

They stumble across the sleeping youths.

But soft, what nymphs are these?

I wonder of their being here together.

Egeus is puzzled to find the rival youths so close together.

No doubt they rose up early to observe the rite of May.

Egeus, is not this the day that Hermia should give answer of her choice?[4]

It is, my lord.

Go, bid the huntsmen wake them with their horns.

1. the vaward of the day: the early part of the day; the morning.   2. the music of my hounds: Elizabethans placed great importance on the 'music' of a pack when choosing hounds.   3. chiding: barking of hounds.   4. give answer of her choice: say whether she agrees to marry Demetrius, as her father wishes.

1. concord: agreement, peace.　2. hither: to this place.　3. stealth: secret plan.　4. by and by: presently.　5. knit: married. **183**

LOST AND FOUND

The actors are alarmed that Bottom is missing.

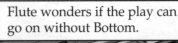

Flute wonders if the play can go on without Bottom.

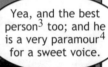

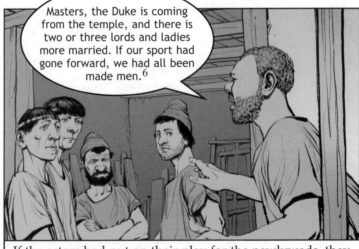

If the actors had put on their play for the newlyweds, they would surely have been paid a great deal of money.

1. transported: carried away, perhaps even dead.   2. marred: spoiled.   3. person: personal appearance.
4. paramour: Quince is confusing 'paramour' (lover) and 'paragon' (a perfect example of something).
5. of naught: shameful.   6. made men: wealthy men.

184

O sweet bully[1] Bottom!

Bottom bursts in, to the joy and delight of the others.

Where are these lads? Where are these hearts?[2]

Bottom! O most courageous[3] day! O most happy hour!

I will tell you every thing, right as it fell out.[4]

Let us hear, sweet Bottom.

Not a word of me. All that I will tell you is, that the duke hath dined.

Bottom has a wonderful story to tell them – or has he?

Get your apparel together, good strings[5] to your beards, new ribbons to your pumps.[6]

Meet presently[7] at the palace; every man look o'er[8] his part: for the short and the long is, our play is preferred.[9]

And, most dear actors, eat no onions nor garlic, for we are to utter sweet breath. No more words: away! Go, away!

There is no time for Bottom's story – they must go straight to the palace to perform their play.

Bottom tells the actors to keep their breath sweet.

1. sweet bully: fine fellow.   2. hearts: good-hearted men.   3. courageous: splendid, magnificent.   4. right as it fell out: just as it happened.   5. strings: to hold their false beards on.   6. pumps: slippers.   7. presently: without delay. 8. look o'er: look over, rehearse.   9. preferred: offered to the Duke, but not yet chosen. Bottom believes it will be chosen.

THE PLAY'S THE THING

'Tis strange, my Theseus, that[1] these lovers speak of.

More strange than true. I never may believe these antique fables,[2] nor these fairy toys.

Here come the lovers, full of joy and mirth!

Theseus and Hippolyta are still puzzled by the story told by the lovers about their night in the wood.

Come now; what masques,[3] what dances shall we have?

Call Philostrate.

Here, mighty Theseus.

Theseus asks for entertainment to fill the evening.

There is a brief how many sports are ripe;[4] make choice of which your Highness will see first.

'A tedious[5] brief scene of young Pyramus and his love Thisbe, very tragical mirth'?

One of the choices is Quince's play.

No, my noble lord, it is not for you: I have heard it over, and it is nothing, nothing in the world.

I will hear that play. Go bring them in.

We will hear it.

So please your grace, the Prologue is address'd.[6]

Let him approach.

Philostrate does not recommend it.

1. that: the thing that.   2. antique fables: absurd stories.   3. masques: plays with music and dancing.
4. a brief how many sports are ripe: a list of the entertainments that are ready.   5. tedious: boring and long-winded; but the actors obviously think it means something else.   6. address'd: ready to begin.

1. This fellow doth not stand upon points: This man doesn't follow punctuation; he doesn't pause in the right places.
2. nothing impaired, but all disordered: nothing broken, but everything out of place; he spoke the words clearly, but they did not make sense.   3. perchance: perhaps.   4. This beauteous lady: Quince promised Flute that he could wear a mask for this part (see page 162), as ancient Greek actors usually did.   5. sunder: split apart.   6. hight: is called.
7. did affright: frightened.

PLAY ON

I, one Snout by name, present a wall; and such a wall as had in it a chink, through which the lovers did whisper often very secretly.

Snout introduces himself to the audience.

I fear my Thisbe's promise is forgot! O wall, show me thy chink, to blink through with mine eyne![1]

Pyramus draws near the wall; silence!

No Thisbe do I see. O wicked wall, curs'd be thy stones for thus deceiving me!

No, in truth sir, he should not. 'Deceiving me' is Thisbe's cue: she is to enter now.

The wall, methinks, being sensible, should curse again.[2]

O wall, full often hast thou heard my moans, for parting my fair Pyramus and me!

I see a voice; now will I to the chink, to spy and[3] I can hear my Thisbe's face. Thisbe?

Wilt thou at Ninny's tomb[4] meet me straightway?

'Tide life, 'tide death,[5] I come without delay.

This is the silliest stuff that ever I heard.

Thus have I, Wall, my part discharged[6] so; and, being done, thus Wall away doth go.

If we imagine no worse of them than they of themselves, they may pass for excellent men.[7] Here come two noble beasts in, a man and a lion.

Hippolyta is unimpressed.

1. eyne: eyes.   2. The wall . . . again: Because the wall has a mind of its own, I think it should curse him back.
3. and: if, whether,   4. Ninny's tomb: Bottom mispronounces 'Ninus' tomb' in Quince's script.
5. 'Tide life, 'tide death: whether life or death results from it.   6. discharged: carried out.   7. If we imagine no worse of them than they of themselves, they may pass for excellent men: If we think of the actors as they see themselves, then they are very good. Theseus may mean that the actors' efforts should be appreciated because they mean well.

Lion warns the audience how frightening he is.

You ladies, you whose gentle hearts do fear the smallest monstrous mouse that creeps on floor, may now, perchance, both quake and tremble here, when lion rough in wildest rage doth roar.

A very gentle beast, and of a good conscience.

This lantern doth the horned[1] moon present; myself the Man i' th' Moon do seem[2] to be.

The man should be put into the lantern. How is it else the Man i' the Moon?

All that I have to say is, to tell you that the lantern is the moon; I, the Man i' th' Moon.

But silence: here comes Thisbe.

This is old Ninny's tomb. Where is my love?

Thisbe can't find Pyramus at their agreed meeting place.

Thisbe drops her cloak as she runs from the lion.

O!

ROAR!!!

The lion rips the cloak to shreds and stains it with blood from a recent kill.

Well roared, Lion!

Well run, Thisbe.

Well shone, Moon! Truly, the moon shines with a good grace.

Well moused, Lion![3]

And so the lion vanished.

1. horned: with points like horns at each end (a crescent moon).   2. seem: pretend.   3. Well moused, Lion!: Theseus compliments the lion on his treatment of the mantle as if he were cat attacking a mouse.

And So to Bed

Pyramus searches for Thisbe by the light of Moonshine.

Sweet Moon, I thank thee for thy sunny beams; I thank thee, Moon, for shining now so bright.

What dreadful dole[1] is here! Thy mantle[2] good, what, stain'd with blood!

He finds Thisbe's blood-stained cloak and assumes the lion has killed her.

Distraught, Pyramus draws his sword and kills himself.

Out sword, and wound the pap[3] of Pyramus; ay, that left pap, where heart doth hop.

Pyramus dies and darkness falls as Moonshine leaves.

Thus die I, thus, thus, thus. Now am I dead, now am I fled; my soul is in the sky.

How chance Moonshine is gone, before Thisbe comes back and finds her lover?

She will find him by starlight.

Hippolyta wonders how Thisbe will find Pyramus's body in the dark.

Asleep, my love? What, dead, my dove? O Pyramus, arise!

Speak, speak! Quite dumb? Dead, dead?

Thisbe kills herself with Pyramus's sword.

Farewell, friends; Thus Thisbe ends: Adieu, adieu, adieu!

Moonshine and Lion are left to bury the dead.

Ay, and Wall too.

190 1. dole: grief.   2. mantle: cloak.   3. pap: breast.

Will it please you to see the epilogue,[1] or to hear a Bergomask dance?[2]

No epilogue, I pray you, for your play needs no excuse.

But come, your Bergomask!

The clock strikes midnight.

The iron tongue[3] of midnight hath told[4] twelve. Lovers, to bed.

'Tis almost fairy time…

I am sent with broom before to sweep the dust behind the door.

Now that everyone is asleep, Puck arrives in the palace.

Through the house give glimmering light by the dead and drowsy fire; every elf and fairy sprite hop as light as bird from briar.

Hand in hand, with fairy grace, will we sing, and bless this place.

To the best bride-bed will we, which by us shall blessed be. So shall all the couples three ever true in loving be.

If we shadows have offended, think but this, and all is mended: that you have but slumber'd here while these visions did appear.[5]

So, good night unto you all. Give me your hands,[6] if we be friends, and Robin shall restore amends.[7]

1. epilogue: a speech to the audience at the end of a play. 2. Bergomask dance: a comic dance in the style of the people of Bergamo in Italy, ridiculed in Shakespeare's time for their rural simplicity. 3. iron tongue: the clapper that strikes the bell of the clock. 4. told: counted. 5. If we shadows . . . appear: If you didn't enjoy the play, just imagine that it was a dream. 6. Give me your hands: applaud. 7. restore amends: make amends in return.

The end

Artists: Penko Gelev

Sotir Gelev

Li Sidong

Nick Spender

Editors: Stephen Haynes, Tanya Kant, Jamie Pitman
Editorial Assistant: Mark Williams

Published in Great Britain in MMXIII by
Book House, an imprint of
The Salariya Book Company Ltd
25 Marlborough Place, Brighton, BNI IUB
www.salariya.com
www.book-house.co.uk

ISBN-13: 978-1-908973-03-0 (PB)

S A L A R I Y A

1 3 5 7 9 8 6 4 2

A CIP catalogue record for this book is available
from the British Library.

Printed and bound in China.
Printed on paper from sustainable sources.

Visit our website at **www.salariya.com**
for **free** electronic versions of:
You Wouldn't Want to be an Egyptian Mummy!
You Wouldn't Want to be a Roman Gladiator!
You Wouldn't Want to be a Polar Explorer!
You Wouldn't Want to sail on a 19th-Century Whaling Ship!

Visit our **new** online shop at
shop.salariya.com
for great offers, gift ideas, all our new
releases and free postage and packaging.